Water

and

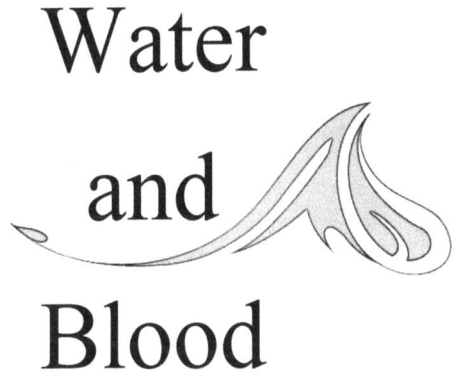

Blood

The Merworld Trilogy

Book 1

B. Kristin McMichael

CONTENTS

CHAPTER 1

Sam didn't look up from his phone as his student swam her laps. He'd been teaching Whitney for over a year now, and she had picked up swimming like she'd been born in the water. He didn't need to watch her; she would be doing the strokes perfectly, as usual. By now she had to be on at least her tenth lap. He doubted she would tire before she got to twenty. For such a scrawny girl, she sure had some muscle.

Whitney made it to the far edge of the pool before Sam snuck at a glance at her. She was far enough away to be safe from his desire to bite into her. No other human had been even half as enticing as she was to him. He had to use all his willpower not to drain her dry each time she had a lesson. Whitney slid through the water effortlessly and was coming closer to where he was seated. Sam had to look down again.

Water splashed a little as Whitney made it to the wall and turned around to go the other direction. Sam pretended there was something on his phone more important than watching her. He didn't need to make any mistakes, like getting obsessed about a girl he could never be with. He was only a senior, but he had been hoping to stay around at least another five or ten years on the mainland. It was expected he would return home to his family eventually, but he wasn't in a hurry to get back to the pressure of all that.

It was taking all his self-control to sit on the side and not jump into the water. His kind wasn't especially known for self-control, either. Sam pressed the buttons on his phone aimlessly.

There was no one calling him, nor would there be. Sirens preferred the island, and not many stayed shoreside for long.

Everyone used the excuse that they needed to head back for something every chance they got. His only other friends were busy with their after-school jobs or getting ready for their next gig. It cost a lot to live on your own. While they pretended to have parents with them, Sam and his friends were really alone, fending for themselves. His second job was at night, and since he didn't need much sleep, it was a good fit.

Sam thought of home to distract himself. It had been over two weeks since he had been back, and he was going to have to make a trip there in the next week or so. They would never let him go too long without checking in. It wasn't that he didn't like the island—it was really pretty perfect—he just wanted to get away. That wasn't possible there. Everyone knew everyone and was in their business. Eventually, he'd have to live there. At some point, the day humans around him were bound to notice he wasn't aging once he turned eighteen in a couple weeks. But until then, he planned to stay on shore as long as he could. It might take moving around a bit, but he was positive he could pull it off until he was at least twenty-five, maybe even thirty.

Whitney splashed again as she turned around and began going the opposite way, her body just breaking the surface as she moved forward and away from Sam again. Sam gripped his phone a little tighter, willing himself to sit still on the bleachers. He couldn't put his finger on why he wasn't able to stay away from this one day human. She was beautiful, but then again so was everyone where he came from. Sirens tended to be as beautiful as the most popular movie stars. It helped when you pretended to save someone in the ocean. Boaters were always much more likely to trust a beautiful face over an ugly one.

His phone beeped as he got a message, and he could concentrate on something other than the human swimming before him. It wasn't much to keep his attention, but he'd read it over a dozen times just to be sure. It outlined the time and place of their gig Friday night. Maybe he could look up where it was. Not that he needed to know; their bus driver would get them there in time. But it would keep him busy for at least another lap. Sam typed the address into his phone and zeroed in on the place. It wasn't too far, only a few hours north. They would be home before sunrise. An easy night. Then again, their manager would want them in the studio if they weren't pulling a late night to record their next album.

Tipping his head back, Sam stared at the clouds. Life would have been much easier if the other night humans knew about the sirens. They would be free to stay on land as much as they wanted, and he would have access to blood banks and not have to trick day humans into swimming lessons to feed himself. And his job of keeping the land sirens safe would be so much easier if they weren't running around hungry all the time. He hated the way everything had turned out. He understood it, but that didn't mean he had to agree.

The splashing in the pool had stopped. Sam looked down to see whether his student was taking a break or she was done for the day. She wasn't at her twentieth lap yet. By his calculations, she was only at fourteen.

Jumping up from his seat, Sam dove effortlessly into the pool and across the width of the lanes without surfacing for breath. Yes, some wandering day human too close to the pool could have seen, but it was an emergency. Whitney was floating face down in the pool, and she wasn't just holding her breath.

In one swift motion, Sam lifted Whitney's lifeless body out of the water as he emerged from below her. He immediately jumped out beside her. Without hesitating, Sam began to breathe into her mouth. Her heartbeat was slowing. He didn't need to feel for a pulse; his senses told him that much. Sam blew into her mouth again, trying to get air to her body.

With her blonde hair matted to her, Whitney lay there limp and unresponsive. Sam stared at her. Even on the verge of death, he was pulled to her, but now his siren instincts were taking over. He had seen his share of people dying from drowning, and they all looked as appetizing as she did when she swam. Now as she was dying Sam realized he didn't want to feed on her, he wanted to keep her alive.

He didn't stop to think about what he was doing as he bit down on his wrist. Blood began to drip down his arm. Placing his wrist over her open mouth, he let only a few drops fall into it. Night human blood was powerful and held healing capabilities for day humans; his would be enough to keep her from dying. At least he hoped so. He had only known of two people ever that used their blood to heal a day human. It had been successful in both getting the human healed and the siren exiled from the island. Sam knew there could be a price if anyone ever found out, but that didn't matter to him. For some reason, keeping the fragile day human in his arms alive was worth it.

Whitney began to cough, and he quickly turned her to her side as she puked out the water stuck in her lungs. Sam licked away the blood on his arm and was thankful for his quick healing abilities as there wasn't a mark left on him.

Wiping her hair out of her face and into something a little more stylish, Whitney pushed herself up to sitting.

"I thought I was taking these lessons so I wouldn't almost drown," she complained.

Sam shook his head. "Then how about next time you come up for a breath instead of trying to make it all the way down the pool like some sort of fish?" Sam replied, easily bantering with her as his own heartbeat slowed down from the excitement. Relief flushed over him, but he pretended like everything was normal.

That was what had happened the last time she almost drowned, except this time technically she did drown. However, Sam wasn't about to correct her. The less she knew, the better.

Whitney ran her hands through her hair again and gave it an easy, perfect twist.

"Fine. I guess I'm not a fish, but wouldn't swimming be much easier if you didn't have to breathe while doing it?"

Sam smiled as she stood up. How true that was.

"Done for today?" he asked as she made her way over to her towel on the sideline.

"Yeah, only one 'almost drowning' per day for me. I'm up to what, four dinners now?"

That was their deal. Since Whitney didn't pay Sam for the lessons, the school did. The first time she had almost drowned, Sam was in the water with her and just had to push her to the edge. That was the first week of class when she thought she was ready to jump in the deep end. She promised to buy him dinner to make up for his saving her. That was five times ago. She was getting better. In fact, it had been months since the last 'almost drowning.'

Whitney wiped the water off her thighs and then her legs. Sam was disappointed. He blamed his siren side, which seemed to be more attracted to women drenched like wet cats than the ones made up with perfect hair and makeup like he had seen on the girls he'd taken on the few land dates he had gone on.

"I think that was six," Sam corrected.

Whitney wrapped her towel around her, completely hiding her body from his view. Sam kept his expression in the normal smile that hid all his thoughts. It was an especially good trick for dealing with her. He focused on her eyes, which were blue, just like the sky. It was harder to keep his gaze from roaming, but everything seemed harder when dealing with Whitney.

"Fine. Six dinners. But you're going to have to wait. I just started my new job, so I won't get paid for two weeks."

"Guess you'll have to stop trying to drown." Okay, he couldn't help that one. It was like Whitney was there to give him a challenge, either in the water or just in a conversation.

"Well, maybe I need a teacher who can show me how to swim without needing air," she kidded back. She was never going to get a new teacher. Only four students at the school taught lessons; he had made sure none of them would agree to teach her so that she had to come to him instead. He would never admit it to another night human that he had a crush on a day human, but by being her teacher, he could spend at least a little time alone with her without any suspicion from anyone.

"Or maybe you'll finally realize you aren't a fish and learn to breathe like everyone else when they swim."

Whitney smiled at him, and Sam would swear it sparkled in the sun.

"You just wait. One of these days I will swim the length of the pool in one breath. You just wait, buddy." Whitney tapped a finger on his chest as she challenged him before turning on her heels and walking away. She gave him a wave as she walked back toward the gate that led into the school locker rooms. She didn't even turn around.

Sam watched her hips sway as she walked. If any other human made that statement, he would have laughed, but Whitney… she was different. It was very possible she would do just that.

The door to the locker room shut, and she was finally out of his view. Sometimes he wished he was a djinn instead of a siren. Then he would grant his own wish and turn Whitney into a night human and he could keep her to himself forever.

Whitney hit the snooze button on her alarm for the tenth time or so. She was beyond tired. Her new job started, and she wasn't yet talented enough to multitask as a waitress. She was going to have to stop dropping stuff and stop talking so much with customers. At least it had been her first week of work, and people were forgiving. Next week might not go as well if she didn't step up and do better. It stunk that her inheritance was locked in a bank account she couldn't access until she was twenty-one. She had to work for any spending money for the next three years.

The alarm beeped again. Swatting at it, Whitney managed to turn it off. She was having a good dream, and the noise was completely ruining it.

Whitney waited for the slumber to come back. She was warm and cozy; it wouldn't take long.

"Leaving in five," Ben, Whitney's younger cousin and ride to school, called from the other side of her shut door.

Her eyes shot open, and she looked across the room at her second clock, which was supposed to have gone off an hour ago, forcing her to get out of bed. It was blinking midnight. They had lost power again, and she still didn't have batteries in it.

Quick mode was going to have to work. Whitney jumped out of bed and slipped into the closest polo shirt she could find in her closet and the khaki skirt from yesterday. One nice thing about a dress code was picking out her clothes was easy when it needed to be. Her hair was a mess from sleeping on it wet after swimming the night before, but that would have to wait. She didn't have time to shower and blow-dry her hair. She barely had time to put on lip gloss as she heard her cousin march by her room and jump down the steps outside her door two at a time. She grabbed her backpack and her shoes to chase after him. He had been threatening for weeks to leave without her, but she didn't want the day she woke up late to include showing up in a thrown-together outfit that was all sweaty from having to jog to school.

Ben walked through the kitchen to the garage and Whitney followed, grabbing an apple on the way. She would rather have time to sit down, eat and maybe even drink some coffee to wake up, but an apple was going to have to do for now.

Out the door and hopping in his car, Ben didn't look back to see if she was there. Whitney kept up with her younger cousin and jumped in the passenger side as the car purred to life.

"I swear you sleep more than a cat," Ben muttered as she sat beside him.

Whitney grinned. She was kind of fond of cats, but that was back when she lived with her family. Her grin faded as it always did when she thought of the home she no longer had.

"Rough swim lesson or rough day at Bingos?" Ben asked.

Whitney had returned home from swimming to get dressed and head right to work. If she had to pick, they were equal in difficultness since she had almost drowned in her lesson right before heading to work.

"Both," she replied, biting into the apple and holding it in her teeth while she reached back and pulled her hair into a sloppy—but would work until she could find a mirror—braid.

"You do know if you'd just go on a date with Mark, I'm sure he'd be easier at Bingos," Ben suggested.

Mark was a senior in their school. He'd been working at Bingos for almost four years and was now an assistant to the manager that ran the place. He had let Whitney know that he was more than willing to date her, but she just couldn't bring herself to say yes. It wasn't his fault. He was cute, with blond, wavy hair that was sun-streaked from hours of surfing, and crystal blue eyes. They would've made a cute matching couple, what with Whitney's own blond hair and blue eyes, but she still couldn't do it. She just didn't see him as boyfriend material.

"Mark isn't the problem," Whitney replied to her cousin. *I am*, she thought.

Ben shrugged. "Either way, it wouldn't hurt anything to just try."

Whitney glowered at her cousin as he drove. He was on

Team Mark since he practically idolized the senior who was the captain of the swim team Ben desperately wanted to be on. Ben spent almost all his free time following Mark around like a puppy, and Mark didn't seem to mind at all. At least Mark was nice enough to put up with Ben, but that didn't make her want to date him either.

"I'm not dating Mark to make him like you better."

Now it was Ben pouting. Whitney turned away from him. From this angle Ben looked so much like her little brother, it made her sad. Her brother was still back home where Whitney wanted to be, but she would never fit in again since their parents died. She had been rightfully shipped off to her aunt to start over when his best friend took him in. She missed him greatly. Starting over would have been so much more fun if her brother was there, but she understood. She only had a year left of school before she would be off to college, and then she would be gone. He had three years of high school left and wanted to be with his friends back home. Knowing that didn't make her miss him any less.

"Hey, don't blame me. I'm only trying to help," Ben said, misunderstanding her sadness.

Whitney turned back to him, shaking her head to get rid of the sad memories and to say no to Ben at the same time.

"I'm still not dating him."

Ben let out a frustrated sigh as he pulled into the school parking lot and drove through to the sophomore lot. Whitney hopped out before he turned off the car.

"Thanks for the lift, cuz," she yelled as she walked quickly to the school. If she got to her locker with enough time, she could stop by the bathroom and make sure she looked okay before class.

Whitney ducked and bobbed through the full hallway to her locker. It had been more than a year ago that her life had changed with the loss of her mother and father, but she was finally getting used to Florida.

"Overslept?" her next door locker mate, Tina, asked.

"Can you tell?" Whitney threw her bag in her locker.

"Only because you're wearing your 'I didn't have time to fix my hair' braid."

Whitney's hands went to her head to pat down the braid and make sure it felt okay. She was never like that at home. She was always on time and styled perfectly, but something with the move threw everything off. At least she kept her room clean still, and that helped with her endless 'not waking in time for school' moments. Whitney blamed it on the heat. Her old home in Washington State was nothing like Florida regarding heat, and she missed it. It was the middle of winter, and she was sweating. There was also the difference in time zones. That had to be it, too.

The bell rang once for a warning. She didn't have time to go check herself. It would have to wait until later.

"Meet you at lunch?" Tina asked.

"Always," Whitney replied.

The school she transferred to was much larger than the one back home where everyone knew everyone since most started kindergarten together. She had moved into that school in eighth grade and started over as the only new person in years. Here, no one seemed to notice or care that there was a new person as it seemed like every month there was someone new.

Whitney made it through her first four classes without finding a single moment to get to the bathroom to check her hair and put on some makeup. It didn't matter too much. Tons of people at school went without any since half of them spent their free time at the beach or in the hot sun. They all looked perfect as it was. Whitney enjoyed the no-fuss vibe of the people around her, and that might have been the reason she was sleeping in more and more.

The crowd all headed toward the lunchroom, and Whitney moved with the flow of bodies. It didn't take long to spot Tina waiting at the end of the hallway near the lunch line. Her dark hair and thick glasses hid the beauty of the girl behind them, making her very distinctive-looking. Whitney had asked more than once why not get contacts, but Tina had no reason other than that she liked her glasses.

"Hot lunch or salad?" Trudy asked as she slid next to Whitney, appearing out of nowhere. She was Whitney's other best friend at her new school.

"Smells good. What is it today?" Whitney asked as she took a whiff of the food coming from the open doorway.

Trudy placed her hand on Whitney's forehead. "Are you feeling okay?"

Scrunching her eyes, Whitney looked at her red-headed friend in confusion. "Um, yeah?"

"It's fish," Tina explained, swatting her friend's hand from Whitney who was still confused.

"Nah, can't be," Whitney replied, walking inside the door and near enough to see the sign posted. "I hate fish and the smell of it."

Sure enough, the sign said fish. Whitney was more confused than before. It really did smell good.

"Did you hit your head at swimming yesterday?" Trudy asked, still searching for a reason for the change.

She linked her arm in Whitney's and pulled her to the salad line. Really, fish wasn't an option for Whitney, and they all knew it. Whitney was tempted to protest. Her friends actually liked fish but refrained from eating it in front of her ever since the first week of school when she puked from the sight of it. They seemed to make fish at least twice a week here. Living by the ocean had some problems. The guys they sat with—Noah and James—actually found her dislike of fish hilarious and liked to use it to tease her. Thankfully, she was in line with the girls who had sympathy with her instead.

"I did almost drown again," Whitney commented. Her friends knew about all the other times, too, and it made them laugh. "This time, Sam actually had to get in the water and not just pull me to the side."

Trudy covered her mouth in a fake gasp, making her deep red curls bounce.

"Prince Sam got in the water to save you? As in, he got wet? That has to be a first."

Whitney giggled. Her friends all called Sam and his friends royalty, and Sam was the prince of them. It actually fit really well. Everyone in his group always looked to him before answering anything. She caught on quickly when she moved there that there were two distinct groups of kids at school—her friends and those that fit in with Sam's royalty group.

"He wasn't even mad," Whitney replied. "But now I owe him six dinners. At this rate, I'll be buying him dinner all summer long."

Pouring dressing over her salad, Whitney made it to the end of the line.

"Uh-oh," Tina said as she poked Whitney in the back. "I think he must have heard us talking about him."

Whitney handed her card to the teacher swiping meals, and pretended to look at her while really looking over the lady's shoulder. Sure enough, Sam was watching her. Even the blonde next to him couldn't get his attention. Whitney stepped a little to the side to be hidden from his view. It made her heart pound to catch him staring like that. Sam was just as gorgeous as the rest of the royalty group that also included her Cousin Ben's favorite person, Mark, but there was something more about the dark-haired leader of the group. Something Whitney couldn't put her finger on.

"Hide me," Whitney pleaded with her friends. She had never once been shy around guys, and when she was alone with Sam, Whitney had no problems talking with him. But when he was with his friends, it was different for some reason.

"Like we could do that," Trudy replied. That much was true. Both Trudy and Tine were more than five inches shorter than Whitney's five foot nine inches.

"Fine. But let's change the subject before he really does hear us." Whitney kept her gaze on her friend and not the set of eyes she felt still watching her.

"That I can do," Trudy replied, knowing how nervous Sam made Whitney. "Just promise me to look at the floor as you walk; we don't want a repeat of last year."

Whitney glanced up at her friend and made a sour pout. They were never going to let her live it down, her dislike of fish. That's what friends were for.

Whitney was thrilled to be back home. She had almost an hour before her shift started at work, and that was enough time to finally get a shower in, after she picked up her room that she'd nearly finished cleaning last night and meant to that morning before she had left in a rush that morning.

Turning on the radio in her room, Whitney hung her bag behind the door, homework and all, and glanced around. It wasn't that messy, especially for a teen. She had seen her friends' rooms over the years, and she was embarrassed when people came to hers and found her room spotless. At least her old best friend understood and never complained at her need for order.

The bed was first on the list. Whitney pulled the sheets up and then the pale pink comforter, which she didn't really need in the heat, and tucked them both in. Without thinking, she leaned over and fluffed the pillows also. The floor was next. She had a few shirts that missed the laundry basket. Her hamper was getting close to half full, so she'd have to do laundry over the weekend.

The radio blasted as she walked around putting everything back in place. Her favorite song began to play, and Whitney couldn't fight the urge to sing along. She was sure her aunt was working, and only her cousin was home. He already, on more than one occasion, had heard her terrible singing. Therefore she didn't care as she began to belt out the song. Whitney danced along as she sang and picked up. Her room was going to be spotless before the song was done, so she moved to her attached bathroom. She could still hear the music.

Whitney continued to sing as she stripped off her school shirt and leaned back into her room to toss it in her dirty laundry hamper.

Shrieking, Whitney ran over to her now open bedroom door.

"Get out of here, Ben," she yelled at her cousin, who was standing with his back to her. Ben didn't move or turn around.

Whitney grabbed a clean towel from the bar inside the bathroom and wrapped it around her top half before marching into her room, hitting the music off on the way. She pulled on her cousin's shoulder to yell at him again; Ben didn't budge.

In the silence of the room, an eerie feeling came over Whitney. She carefully walked around her cousin to see him staring straight ahead with a dazed expression on his face. His eyes focused on nothing, and his mouth hung slightly open. He looked like a statue, and if it wasn't for the small movements of his chest, she wouldn't even know if he was alive.

"Ben?" Whitney asked, all anger gone. Something beyond weird was going on. Whitney reached up and gently touched his face. "Ben. Are you in there?"

Still, there was no movement from him, or any kind of recognition.

Reaching for her phone, Whitney never took her eyes off Ben. Something wasn't right, and she had no idea what it meant. The only thing she could think to do was call her friends back home. They dealt a lot with weirdness, and she had to hope they could tell her what to do.

As she pressed the first digit of her best friend's phone number, Ben snapped out of his daze.

"What the heck, cuz? You know I don't need to see you walking around in a towel," Ben complained in true brotherly fashion as he came to.

"Um, then don't come in my room ..."

Whitney was still unsure about what had just happened, but she stopped dialing since he seemed to be better now and she wanted to believe everything was perfectly fine. It had to be her imagination. She had been away from the night human world and all the weirdness that went with it for over a year. She was just a normal day human, and odd things didn't happen to day humans. She had to believe that.

Ben glanced around the room and then reached up to scratch the back of his head. He didn't seem to understand what he was doing either, but at least he was back mentally and not just a statue.

"Um yeah," he said as he turned to leave, just as confused as Whitney was.

Whitney set her phone down and closed her bedroom door, turning the lock as she did so. She wasn't having a repeat since she needed to get a shower. She would have yelled more at him, but it was just too strange, and he didn't seem to have done it on purpose. Whitney could write off all the weird things in her life easily, as there were hundreds of reasons behind them, all pointing back to the world she left behind, but Ben had never been part of the night human world. He was just a human through and through.

Spending most of her life in a world filled with people that needed to drink blood would normally sound crazy, but that had been her life. She had once been one and even felt the urge to bite someone for the warm, red liquid. Night humans were everywhere. She understood there was so much in the world connected to them, even if most day humans never knew they existed.

Making her way back to the bathroom, Whitney hung her towel up and stripped off the rest of her school clothes. She turned the water on and didn't check to see if it was the right temperature. Even if she wanted a hot shower, it would do no good. The water heater barely got above warm, and if she did take a hot shower, she would get out and begin sweating more. Whitney really didn't like Florida's hot and humid weather, but she only had to make it through a few more months, and she'd be free to leave.

The white curtain blocked the spray of water as Whitney climbed in and held her breath, ready for the lukewarm water to hit her as the curtain folded back in place. She wasn't prepared for the tingling that started at her toes. Whitney glanced down to see that her legs were fusing together, beginning to form what appeared to be a fin.

Shoot, shoot shoot, Whitney thought as she felt it move further up her legs.

She reached down quickly and plugged the drain. It wasn't her first time transforming into an animal. Before her life had changed, she used to change into a beautiful tawny cat on the full moon. That was the life she missed, but for the past fourteen months, she had been change-free. And she had never turned into a fish before. She had to hope she'd be a big fish and if not the drain would catch her from going in the sewer.

The tingling crept up her body. It felt like a snail's pace as she worried about what it all meant, but in reality it probably only took seconds. Whitney couldn't really tell what was going on as it continued down her arms. Weirdly, she felt tingles, but nothing was happening to her upper body.

They finally stopped, and she stared at where her legs used to be. Reaching to touch the beautiful pink fin with her human hands, Whitney felt the slick scales beneath her fingers. She wasn't changing into a fish. She had a fish tail but that was it... she was a mermaid. Yep, life had just moved past beyond weird, directly to super confusing.

CHAPTER 2

Sam watched from his locker as Whitney made her way down the hallway. He tried to hide his stare as his friends talked around him, but he was still worried. She had been close to death just over twenty-four hours ago, and yet she seemed fine. *Seemed* was the part that bothered him. Whitney was great at "seeming to be" a lot of things. No one saw the tears or the sad eyes she had when she watched the ocean at his favorite surf spot.

The first time Sam had seen Whitney was before he knew who she was or that she would be going to his school. The pier was usually busy, and he hated to be around so many day humans. He had been on land for years, but at times it still got to him. They always smelled delicious. There was a better spot down a ways from the pier, but still within view of it. That was his spot, right after the bend that kept him away from all the non-stop chattering of a world he was never going to be part of, a world on the land and not the sea.

Sam was alone when he spotted her. At first, he thought she was an illusion from the sun shining just right on the sand, but as he got closer, he realized she was real. She never noticed him as he snuck into the water to get closer.

From beneath the waves, he was able to circle around her spot on the rocks of the bend. She was staring in the direction of the pier, and thus he was hidden as he surfaced. Luckily she didn't see him, but there was more than one occasion since that he wished she would have.

"What do you think?" someone asked from beside Sam.

Shaking from his thoughts of Whitney, he realized he was calmer now that he saw her walking into the school and not suffering any lasting effects from his blood. He needn't have worried; she was just as graceful as ever and completely alive.

Sam turned to the voice beside him.

Amber batted her eyes lashes at him. Sam was growing sick of all her advances. They had grown up together, but he had made it very clear that he wasn't choosing a mate until he was forced to. Amber seemed to take that at a challenge, and as his eighteenth birthday approached, she was trying harder to get him to notice her. And he did notice her, but that didn't change anything. She was like a sister to him. They had swum their first times together, learned how to catch fish, climb a tree, and sneak away from the island altogether. He never once saw her as anything but family.

"About?" Sam asked vaguely. He hadn't heard a bit of the conversation as he watched Whitney. He tried to act as if he was just spacing out and not watching the day human none of them ever saw instead.

"Whether we should skip the party also," Amber replied, latching her arm on to his. "I'm voting for staying here with you in protest."

Sam wanted to pull away since Whitney was coming closer, but that would make Amber suspicious. She already was watching each of the people he taught swim lessons to. She constantly told him that the only way he could really tell her *no* on being together was if he found someone else. He almost said he had, but stopped himself before he did.

"I say we should all stay back on land," Leo stated from the other side of Amber.

"I agree," Amber added, fluffing her blond curls with the arm that wasn't hooked on to him.

Amber had the same blond hair and blue eyes, but she still didn't compare to Whitney. Her arm holding him in place couldn't make his heart beat faster like Whitney could do with just a glance. Sam had no idea how else he could get through to Amber that he was never going to choose her. She was either too dense to understand or didn't want to. It was more than likely the latter.

"No. You guys will all get in trouble. My father called everyone back. You can't defy him without getting him upset. Heck, if you all stayed, he might be upset enough to exile you guys," Sam repeated what he had explained the week before and the week before that. It was great that they all wanted to have his back with him defying his father, but he couldn't let them do it. He would get in enough trouble as it was.

"But if you aren't going to be there, then what's the point?" Mark asked.

"The party will go on with or without me. Me showing up won't make a difference," Sam replied. And it was true. It wasn't like his father would ask him his thoughts on anything. He never did. Sam was to be the obedient son. That was his role.

Whitney had her books in her hands now and was walking back past them on her way to her science class. Sam's class was right next door. Quickly, he reached into his locker and grabbed his own books.

"You guys will attend, as my father asked. That's the last of it," Sam ordered them.

Sulking, Amber nodded her head. She had no choice when Sam commanded it. That was the only perk of being the head of the guard. Everyone, beyond his brothers and father, had to listen to him. His friends, even though meaning well, would be at the party he was going to avoid. They would be safe, and he would have done his job yet again.

Sam untangled his arm from Amber as gracefully as he could, hopefully without angering her, and made his way down the hallway after Whitney. She had paused at her friend's locker. He slowed to stay behind her. He wasn't sure if he had been caught watching her by anyone, but he kind of suspected a few times she had caught him. It was easier to stay behind to not get caught another time. They took off toward the science building, and he kept pace with them, listening just a little to their conversation. Whitney was unusually quiet, and that worried him. Something was up. He had followed her around long enough to know, around friends, Whitney was never quiet.

Whitney slipped into her classroom, and Sam slowed down to be able to catch a glimpse from the doorway. She was already seated and staring off into space. Her eyes were distant, as were her thoughts. Sam was getting worried. Could the blood have done something bad to her? Was she feeling sick? He would never forgive himself if his blood had hurt her. He didn't know what to expect, but at least she was alive. Her heart beat loudly as he walked past the room. She sounded healthy from what he heard, and the color was completely back in her cheeks, but it still worried him. She was never quiet and pensive at school. That was always left at the beach. He had wished a hundred times he could ask her about that, but then it would give away that he saw her there, and she might actually look for him.

Sam sighed as he turned to his own classroom. The bell was going to ring soon, and he couldn't just stand in the hallway watching her. The draw of Whitney was as strong as ever. Sam was never going to be with Amber or any other person as long as Whitney was alive, and no one could ever know that was the real reason.

Whitney was beyond happy for it to be Friday. She needed the weekend, and she needed it badly. Her life had completely turned upside down. Her shower the night before was weird, but as soon as she turned it off and dried off, her legs reappeared. It had been a pain to get that large fin out of the tub to dry it off, but she did it and then had legs again. She really had no clue what it all meant. Mermaids weren't real. Well, at least everything she had been told growing up had led her to believe that they weren't.

Lessons in night human history were required in all the different night human territories. From what she had been taught, there had been merpeople at some point, but they had all died in the war between the night humans that had happened hundreds of years ago. She was certain of it. Yes, werewolves and vampires were real, but not mermaids. Everyone knew that. Well, everyone except her legs that had melted together into a fin when she tried to take a shower. At least she hadn't completely turned into a fish like she was afraid would happen. She used to be a skinwalker that completely turned into a mountain lion, so anything was possible. Being part fish was easier to work with than being a whole fish, hopefully.

Why she had changed was the mystery. She needed time to figure it all out. There was no reason for her turning into a mermaid that she could come up with. And she wasn't craving blood either. All night humans craved blood. So now she felt more like it was just her imagination playing with her. Maybe her blood sugar was low, and it had all been a hallucination.

She was left with too many questions to pay attention in school. Swimming in thoughts from the night before and trying to remember every little detail from her childhood when she learned about merpeople, her head wasn't making sense of anything she had been taught all morning. It really was a good thing that it was Friday. She had completely checked out of school mentally already. After lunch, she was sure to not have any more luck with her classes since she was completely preoccupied and those classes were really boring without her mind elsewhere.

Whitney vaguely listened to her friend Tina fight with her twin brother, Noah. Noah had the same dark hair and glasses as his twin, but stood almost a foot taller than her five-foot-two frame. Luckily their argument was over a comment made in the only class they had together, and Whitney wasn't taking calculus, so she didn't need to chime in. Instead, she used the time to glance around the room.

There was no sure way to become a night human unless your parent was one. Whitney's mother was a witch, but not a night human. Only a day human could do magic, and since her mother was good—really good—at being a witch, Whitney knew that there was no hidden night human merperson blood coming from her. Whitney's father was a completely different story. He was a night human, but not a mer. After her parents and a stranger had died tragically, she found out the second man with them was actually her birth father. It hadn't taken any convincing for Whitney. She saw herself in his face. They looked more alike than she and her mother. She knew nothing about her mysterious father, and there could have been a secret, hidden merperson history. That was most likely not true either, though, since she had already been a night human. You could only be one kind. Whitney was pretty sure there were no hidden mermaid genes from him, either, that popped up over her vacation from the night human world. Skinwalkers and wendigo stayed only with their own kinds, too.

Then again, there was one more very slim chance of a way to become a night human—night human blood. Whitney had heard of this, but she had never actually seen it. The skinwalkers were born, not changed, but other night humans grew their clan by changing people, or so she had been told. While she lived mostly outside of the politics, she had heard her share over dinner conversations about it. That, too, was a problem, though. From the little bit she had heard, the person changing had to know, and be willing to change. Along with that, you needed powerful night human blood. Not everyone in the clan could change someone, only the people on top. Was it possible she had met a strong night human mermaid that had put a spell on her, and who forced her to drink their blood and change?

Whitney rifled through all her recent memories. She

really had no idea how else she could have become a mermaid the night before. She considered calling her friends back home, but then thought against it. Her best friend was mated to the clan's beta, who was next in line for alpha. He would have no choice but to tell the alpha, and then she would be in for the treat of finding out what they did with night humans that shouldn't exist. Yes, Whitney wanted to go home, but she didn't want to go back as a prisoner or to a science lab to be studied.

Being raised a witch made Whitney a very cautious person. She couldn't think how someone would have been able to change her without her knowing. Changing a person into a night human took blood, and Whitney was sure she had never drunk blood as a day human. Some people would use night human blood to heal since it could heal a day human from most injuries, but she had never been hurt or even to the hospital in her life before. There was no way she could have accidentally drank blood.

"You think, just because you are a stupid boy, you should save me," Tina complained to her brother, pulling Whitney out of her thoughts as her braid whipped around her head and smacked into Whitney.

Tina's words resonated in Whitney's mind. Her head snapped up, and she glanced across the lunchroom. She might not have drank blood on purpose, but there were five times that she could count where she was unconscious long enough that someone could have given her blood. And there was only one person that someone could be. Across the lunchroom, a pair of golden brown eyes stared back at her as the girl next to him chattered away to him. Sam was watching her.

His eyes were always unsettling to Whitney. The color was brown most of the time, but it always seemed like if she stared long enough, the brown color would get lighter and actually turn a bit blue-green. This had unnerved Whitney the first time she saw it happen, and she tried not to look too long at him, afraid that her overactive imagination would be correct. Now she didn't avert her gaze. He was the key to it all. She was certain of that.

Sam's eyes never left Whitney as she stared back at him, trying to understand her own thoughts. He was possibly a night human. He probably wasn't the only one, but he was the only person alone with her long enough to have fed her blood. She wasn't sure she believed it. Who had ever heard of a male mermaid? Weren't mermaids 'maids,' after all?

Someone leaned down in front of Sam, blocking Whitney's view of him.

"Is Prince Sam still giving you crap about saving you?" Tina asked quietly from beside Whitney. She had been staring and didn't notice that the argument between Tina and her brother was done.

"No. But I still owe him meals," Whitney added. *That's it!* She could invite him to dinner and throw some water on him. Then she'd be able to tell.

Whitney picked at her food and pretended to not be keeping tabs on Sam. Throw water on him? That idea wouldn't work. She had already seen in him the water on more than one occasion. He was her swim instructor. He didn't have a fin. But maybe he knew who did. It wasn't uncommon for day humans to be able to get ahold of night human blood if you knew the right people. He could have night human blood on hand to save people when he was life guarding. It didn't matter that he wasn't one of them; he might know one. Whitney had to talk to him.

"Hey. You could always buy him McDonald's and give it to him at your swim lesson next week. That's dinner, right?" Tina suggested, thinking Whitney's disappointment was from owing Sam dinner.

"Yeah, you won't use up your first paycheck that way," Trudy chimed in from across the table. She was always good about ignoring the guys sitting with them, and even better when Tina was fighting with her brother. They were more like sisters than friends.

Whitney smiled at her friends. It was a good idea, but she couldn't wait until her next swimming lesson. She needed to talk to him now.

"Who's that with Sam?" Whitney asked as casually as she could.

A dark-haired stranger that looked similar to Sam was standing next to him in the middle of the lunchroom. Whitney didn't know all the people at the school, but she was sure he wasn't a student even though he seemed like he could fit right in.

"Sam's older brother, Tim," Trudy replied. "You think everyone does what Sam wants, look at how they are all waiting to do anything for Tim. It was much worse two years ago when Tim was in school. Sam isn't even an ounce of bossy compared to his brother."

That was the first compliment Trudy had given Sam. Most of the time Whitney's friend didn't talk too nicely about him. Maybe that was part of her fear to speak to Sam in front of everyone. Normally she wouldn't care what her friends thought, but with being new, she was just happy to have friends and fit in.

Tim spoke, and Sam's face turned to a scowl. Everyone around them was watching Tim and Sam even though Tim didn't seem to notice. Sam put a hand up to stop Tim from talking more and walked away. Tim smiled at the people at the table and followed behind Sam as he left the lunchroom. Whitney didn't want to let Sam out of her sight. So far she figured that he wasn't a mermaid, but that didn't mean he wasn't the one who turned her. The more she thought about it, the more she was sure Sam had something to do with it.

"Not fair," Noah complained to their other friend, James, waving his arm and knocking over his water.

It was strange. Whitney could have sworn that she heard the water swoosh in the air as it made its way to the table and toward her. Without hesitation, Whitney stood up quickly before any of the water could touch her and accidentally make her grow a fin.

"I'll go get more napkins," she suggested, hurrying away and avoiding the close call.

She had experimented the night before and found the fin only appeared if the lower half of her body got wet. Right now she was in her school skirt and would easily have wet legs if she hadn't moved. Actually, she would have had a wet fin.

As she turned the corner to the lunch line supplies that were stacked neatly and had all the extra paper towels, the voices of two people arguing grew louder. They weren't in the same hallway, but around the corner. Whitney crept forward; all her years in cat form were very helpful in keeping completely silent.

"So what if you don't want to come home? He wasn't asking you," one voice said.

"If Dad wants to give an order, tell him to come here and do that. Until then, I'm busy," the other replied. Sam was the second person talking.

"He hasn't been here in years. That's what he has us for."

"Are you sure? I figured he had us because he can't seem to keep everyone safe on his own, and it's easier to sacrifice a son than lose his throne." Footsteps sounded as one of them seemed to be walking away. They halted before Whitney needed to find a place to hide.

"He's heard a rumor you plan to revolt, that there are several more blues who plan to skip the party." Tim's voice was soft but harsh as he spoke. "You are playing with fire, little brother. I'd advise you to not go down that road. Father can forgive almost anything, but if you plan to overthrow him, you'd better hope I'm not alive when you do."

"Thanks for the advice, but you might want to be a bit more worried what father might have heard about you," Sam replied back as harshly as his brother. "Just because I'm not home doesn't mean I don't know what's going on."

A loud laugh made Whitney jump and almost give away her sneaking around.

"Ahh, little brother, you're so much fun. I can't wait until you move home. It will be just like old times."

Footsteps sounded again, and this time, Whitney grabbed the napkins and fled back around the corner. Hurrying over to her friends, she discovered the water was still on the table but not dripping. Whitney tossed the napkins on the water.

"Thanks," Noah said, giving her a sheepish smile for his klutziness as he wiped up his mess.

Whitney nodded and tried not to watch as Sam came back around the corner behind his brother. Tim had a smile plastered on his face as he walked over to Sam's table and sat down in Sam's seat. Sam wasn't in the same jolly mood. Whitney caught Sam's eyes before quickly looking away. She wasn't close enough to see for sure, but they didn't look brown. Sam was hiding more secrets, and she was sure he was the one that knew what was going on with her. Now she just needed to get him alone and force him to tell her what he had done to her.

Whitney made up the worst excuse about needing to use the restroom just to get out of the last five minutes of class. Her face was flushed red from embarrassment, especially since she didn't really need to go at all and never had needed to bad enough to interrupt class! Instead of heading to the bathroom like she asked, she grabbed her books out of her locker just in time for the bell to ring to end the day. Without saying good-bye to anyone, Whitney hurried off in the direction of Sam's locker. Passing him on her way, she tried to not look at him and give herself away. She turned the corner near enough to peek around, and then pretended she needed to search through her backpack.

Students passed Whitney and didn't take notice of her there as they ran from the school, a typical Friday afternoon.

She kept her spot where she would see Sam again as he passed. Sure enough, ten minutes later, Sam walked right by. Whitney kept tabs on him and followed him out of the school. She was relieved to see Sam not head toward the parking lot. She hadn't thought about what she would do if he just took off in a car after school. She didn't have a car, and it would be impossible to follow him on foot. Thankfully, he was still walking with his friends

Whitney kept her head down as her cousin texted her to tell her he was leaving without her. She responded that she would get a ride home later from a friend. She really didn't care if she had to walk home. She needed answers and wasn't letting her only source of them out of her sight.

Sam and Mark went around the school together and walked off the school grounds. Whitney kept pace, but stayed hidden as she did so. She had no idea where they were going. There was nothing that direction out of town besides a few warehouses, but she didn't care. She needed Sam.

The boys talked as they walked, seemingly like they were in no hurry. As they turned and headed toward one of the warehouses, Whitney stayed outside the chain-link fence and crouched behind the old board with the address on it. Peeking around the corner with her phone, she watched as Sam and Mark walked onto a waiting bus. They were only on the bus for a few moments before they stepped back off. Whitney had no clue why a large bus was sitting outside a rundown building, but it was something she planned to look closer at. Once they exited and walked into the building, Whitney didn't hesitate to move closer to be able to hear them if they came back outside. She hid behind the bus.

They weren't inside long before a car pulled up to the warehouse and their friend Leo stepped out of it. He went inside where Sam was. Whitney waited, unsure if she should try to go in or wait for them to come out.

The door to the building slammed open, and the guys

came back out. She could hear them as they talked. She was in a much better spot to figure it out now.

"How far away this time?" Leo asked, almost like he was complaining.

"If I was driving? We could be there in three hours, but you know how Mr. Max drives. It will probably take him at least five hours to get there," Mark complained.

They were going somewhere, but where was the question. Whitney couldn't afford to let Sam escape. What if he didn't come back?

There was a *thunk* from the other side of the bus that made Whitney curious. She whipped her phone back out and looked around the vehicle. The guys were all packing something into the storage spots beneath the big bus. They were definitely going somewhere and taking large bags with them.

"This would be much easier if we'd just let them send a crew to load all our stuff up," Mark replied. For as smooth as he was when talking to Whitney, she was surprised to see the complainer side of him. Nothing at work seemed to ever bother him.

"But we all agreed not to. It is safer for us this way," Sam reminded his friend. "So we pack."

All three guys headed back into the gray, worn-down building. Whitney didn't think, but used their absence as an opportunity. If the guys were going somewhere on the bus, then she was going with them. The bus was big enough. She could just hide in a row of seats and hope they didn't walk by. Whitney climbed up the stairs and ducked down as soon as the door opened to the warehouse again. Pressing her back against the panel, she held her breath, hoping they wouldn't come up inside the bus where she wasn't even close to hidden.

They talked more as they packed and soon enough the door to the warehouse opened and shut again. Whitney tentatively stood up, trying to hide as much of herself as she could under the windows. Finally looking around the bus, she was confused by what she saw. She had expected rows of seats. Instead, she found two benches against the windows on either side of the bus, with doors at the back. Whitney half walked, half crawled toward the other end of the bus. She would need a good hiding spot.

Beyond the benches in the first door on the right was a bathroom—basically a small closet with a toilet and sink. Not a good choice for hiding spots. On the left side was a door that led to a shower. The door appeared to open right into the shower; it was a possible hiding spot, but since the bus would be moving, a slippery shower wasn't ideal. She would keep searching.

Whitney glanced out the windows and saw the guys come back out with more equipment. That was just another mystery. *Hiding space first, figuring out what was going on would have to be second.* Whitney slid down and hoped they hadn't seen her.

Voices came through the open bus door as they packed, but instead of coming up, they headed back in. She was safe for now, so she hurried to the back of the bus and stopped in shock. There was what looked like a bathtub in the back of the bus. Prying off the corner of the cover confirmed what she thought it was—a hot tub big enough to fit several people. Certainly not a good hiding spot since any sort of water turned her into a fish. There were bench seats also in the back, but that wouldn't work as she would be in plain view of the bus driver.

Making the way back to the front of the bus, Whitney continued to try to find a hiding spot. She didn't want to get off the bus. She needed to talk to Sam, and if he was going somewhere, she was going with him. *Think, think, think*, she told herself as she tapped her head. While a natural blonde, Whitney was anything but dumb, regardless of all the jokes she had heard over the years. She needed somewhere to hide.

The guys came back out the door, and she dropped to the

ground next to the bench seat. This was never going to work out if they found her. She turned her head and waited as she listened to them talk. Hopefully, they weren't done, as she needed more time to search the bus. There had to be a way to hide. Whitney turned her head toward the bench seat as she listened more. Then she saw it: the bench seats had a cloth running down the front and sides to make them look like solid seats, but they weren't. They were empty underneath.

Whitney scrambled to the end of the bench and pulled up the fabric flap. The guys still hadn't gone back inside, which wasn't good news. She slithered under the seats and luckily they were long enough that she could fit by lying straight as a board. Whitney reached down and grabbed her phone, turning off the ringer just to be safe as she smashed herself as far away from the front of the seat as she could.

Her hiding spot was perfect and perfectly timed as someone came onto the bus. Whitney sucked in her breath and plastered her body as close to the wall as possible, trying to make sure that if the cloth moved a little, she would still be hidden. Three sets of shoes walked past her.

"Where is he?" Mark complained.

"He was just inside. Did anyone tell him we were almost packed?" Sam replied.

"Yeah, yeah, you brats already told me. Can't an old guy take a few minutes longer to get on the bus?" a gruff voice complained as the speaker slowly, but loudly, walked up the stairs.

The seat bounced a little as someone sat down.

"Don't take all day, old man," Leo said to him teasingly. "We still need to perform tonight, and the opening act won't last all evening."

"I'll have you guys there by eight, don't worry about that," the older man replied, shutting the door to the bus with a clank and turning the engine on.

The noise rumbled beneath Whitney, and she could no longer make out the words of the guys. If they were going on a four-hour bus ride, she sure wasn't going to be home by curfew. She needed to make a few texts to make sure she didn't get in trouble. It wasn't like her aunt really would notice. She was probably working, but Whitney didn't want to take the chance she would actually be home and call the cops. She had done that on more than one occasion for her younger cousin. Tina would lie to her aunt and say she was there. Heck, if needed, Tina actually did a really good impression of Whitney that could even fool her aunt.

The bus lurched forward, and Whitney braced herself beneath the seats. It was going to be a long four hours, but at least she would get an answer to one question. What the heck was Sam up to with his friends?

CHAPTER 3

Sam wiped the sweat off his face as he exited the stage. He was hungry and all the control he had to use while singing made it worse. He'd probably have to head right out to sea as soon as they got back to find something to eat. Human blood was preferred and most never strayed, but Sam found he could bear any type of mammal blood if needed. At least the guys understood, or rather tolerated, Sam. Well, they understood that the singing was hard, but heading out to feed would make them upset as always. He was pretty sure they had more than a few treats waiting to ride the bus with them. Sam just didn't feel like feeding on some strangers. Who he really wanted to feed on was a stunning blonde, but she wasn't an option. He had already fed on Whitney that week before when he had to rescue her in her swim lesson. He was limited to drinking blood only once every two weeks from her.

Singing for money wasn't Sam's first choice of professions. He would have been much happier washing cars or being a lifeguard. But those jobs didn't pay nearly as much as singing. And singing kept him off the radar of the hunters. They would never expect him to be a siren since he could sing on stage and not affect the audience. Sam was lucky he had the control. Leo and Mark didn't. Good thing they could play backup, and their manager hired backup singers once Sam had convinced him that Leo and Mark couldn't sing.

"The bus will be packed up in fifteen," Clark said as he tossed Sam a towel. "If you'd let my guys go back with you, they'd have it unpacked just as quick."

Clark, their manager for the past two years, always

offered to send someone back. That was really just code that he wanted to see where Sam and the guys lived and recorded their music. Sam couldn't let him do that. He'd see that they didn't exactly record in a rundown place like he thought. Being a siren did have it's perks, like people willing to donate large amounts of new equipment if you asked nicely, or maybe sang them a song or two. Sam didn't feel like it was right, but then again, at least they didn't kill the day humans to get the equipment, and it wasn't his fault day humans fell for their songs.

Sam climbed up into the bus to wait and stripped off his shirt in the process. He was still drenched in sweat from being on the stage, and the towel around his neck wasn't keeping his shirt dry. They were almost finished packing, and he should have stayed down to make sure everything was packed correctly, but he didn't want to stick around all the day humans who were hanging out and screaming his name. It wasn't exactly safe at the moment now that his hunger was growing.

He could smell the day human guests the guys brought on when he walked on the bus, and ignored them as he sat down in the front. It was going to be torture, four hours of it to be exact. One of these days he was going to have to leave his morals at the door and join them, but not today. He still had enough control to make it home.

Leo walked on the bus behind Sam with his own day human groupie hanging on him.

"Going to join us in the tub?" Leo asked as the girl beside him giggled into his chest. She didn't look like she was old enough to be out as late as it was. Sam raised an eyebrow to Leo, who smirked and wiggled his own eyebrows in return. No, she probably wasn't.

The girl finally noticed Sam where he sat, and she swooned at the sight of him. Sam rolled his eyes at Leo who tried to keep her from falling by pressing her into a hug.

"There's plenty of food if you want to join us," Leo

added. "Mark always picks up at least three."

"No thanks," Sam replied, waving Leo through the bus to the back where the hot tub was.

Leo shrugged and ushered the girl in his arms to the back of the bus. He turned to ask Sam one last time, but Sam just stared back at him, giving him the look that said to keep their feeding safe. The only way Sam even allowed Mark and Leo to feed on the bus was if they made sure their girls wouldn't die and bring attention to their group. Mark had agreed as he was used to Sam and his no-kill policies, but Leo took some arguing with. When they met a hunter at their first concert, Leo seemed to agree that draining their dates was off the table. It was a close enough call for him to reform, at least in front of Sam.

Sam wasn't against killing day humans in particular—they were food after all—but he took his job very seriously. He was responsible for the sirens living in his town. He hated to have to go fight with the hunters. They were trouble and had killed two of his older brothers when they were the head of the guard as Sam was now. By enacting the policy where they wouldn't kill day humans once he came to land at sixteen, Sam had made the sirens on land completely safe. They hadn't had a hunter in town in over eighteen months. Everyone hated the policy, but they agreed it was the best idea. Sam was there to protect them, but he couldn't protect everyone at every moment.

Lying back against the window, Sam let his mind drift. He wouldn't fall asleep on the bumpy bus, but he could daydream a bit. His daydreams went instantly to her as he knew they would. Whitney had been at school today, and since lunch, with his brother showing up, he had noticed her attention on him. He hoped that wasn't because of Tim. Girls always fell for Tim. Sam knew Whitney wasn't like most girls, but she was still just a day human girl. Tim's charms probably would work on her and that kind of upset him. Tim could never be the guy for Whitney. He was rotten to the core. Whitney deserved more than that.

Whitney's new attention on him got him thinking. Part of him wondered if she remembered anything from her swim lesson, but that was impossible. She was almost dead. If she remembered anything, she'd think Sam was part angel. Sam snuck a glance or two at her each time he saw her during the day. Was it possible that she looked more beautiful and alluring than before? She was just a day human and playing tricks on him. It had to be the lack of blood. He needed to take on a few more students to feed from. That's what he needed.

The bus started up, and Sam realized he hadn't noticed the bus driver, Mr. Max, come onboard. Anyone could have come on the bus, and they would have been in trouble if it were a hunter. He was going to have to quit all his daydreaming. He would fail at his job if he was too busy thinking of a particular blonde who invaded his every thought.

Sam sat up as the bus pulled out of the parking lot and turned to head toward home. The boys in the back with their girls were splashing around in the hot tub. He wasn't about to join them. The water splashed again, and Sam stood up. He couldn't risk feeding on the girls, but he could take a shower. There was enough water in the system for two showers, and if he took one long one, he would feel better. His skin had been itching since the afternoon.

One of the girls giggled as Mark began to sing. It was only the first time of the ride they would be feeding. Sam really didn't need to stick around to hear that also. It was bad enough he was craving blood and a certain blonde girl that would never be his. Life overall sucked for the time being. His father wanted him to come home, and he couldn't live the life he wanted if he did that. Yep, life more than sucked. Sam needed a miracle and something to keep him distracted from his life.

Opening the door to the shower, Sam just stood and

stared. He had asked for a miracle, but he hadn't really expected one to be waiting there. Sam wasn't one for organized religion, but perhaps that was about to change. He reached forward and touched the girl in his shower. No, he wasn't just imagining it. Whitney was really there.

Whitney's mouth hung open in shock. She hadn't had time to hide back under the seat after the concert when Mark showed up with two girls in tow. She figured they would need to pack everything, but she saw Mark coming as soon as she was on the bus. She was lucky she made it on at all, and that would have been majorly awkward if she had to get someone to drive up in the middle of the night to get her. She still didn't know exactly where she was. Once on the bus, Whitney ducked into the shower, hoping to move once the coast was clear. Mark had walked on the bus and hadn't left. It was either the shower or the bathroom. She was sure that the bathroom was the more used room, and since none of the guys used the shower on the way to the concert, she took the only chance to make it home unseen. Well, that didn't exactly turn out that way.

Sam didn't say a word as he stared at Whitney. She didn't know what to say either. Was he going to tell the other guys?

Stepping into the already small space, Sam shut the door behind him. His wide shoulders almost touched both sides of the walls at the same time. The plastic walls rattled, and the water perched above Whitney began to fall. She heard the water move just as she had at lunch, but now there was nowhere to go. There was barely enough room for the both of them as it was.

The water fell from the corner above her head, and Whitney only stared at Sam as it happened. She regretted that she was fully dressed and turning into a night human. She was going to have to walk home naked after she dried off, and it was going to be completely humiliating as it was just to turn back in front of the guys. She didn't need to look; she could feel her legs melt together. What she needed was for Sam to tell her what the heck was going on. From the expression on his face, he was shocked, but not the kind of shock like he hadn't seen a fin or two before.

"Care to explain?" Whitney asked from her seat in the shower. How nice that the shower had a small bench seat. She didn't have to tip over like she did in her own shower when it first happened.

"Crap," Sam replied. That wasn't an explanation at all.

"Buddy, you're missing all the fun," Mark yelled, pounding on the door. Sam had locked it behind himself, but the flimsy plastic wobbled.

Sam put a finger to his mouth for Whitney to be quiet. Even though she had no idea what was going on, she nodded. For some crazy instinct, she trusted Sam.

"I'm not hungry. I plan to shower and use up all the water," Sam told his friend. That must have been a good enough answer since he seemed to relax, like Mark was now gone again.

Sam reached past Whitney and turned the nozzles to the shower.

Whitney would have "eeked" at the cold water that was shooting out of the shower head, but it didn't feel cold at all. It actually felt nice. Sam moved closer into the small amount of room in front of Whitney and looked down at her. Bracing his hands on either side of her head, he moved his face beside hers.

"I'm going to pick you up and set you on my lap," he explained in a calm voice, like he might upset her.

Whitney didn't like to be manhandled, but then again, there wasn't much she could do with a fin, and since he turned the shower on, the fin wasn't going anywhere.

Sam easily picked her up and maneuvered himself to the seat beneath her with her back on his lap. Whitney grabbed around his neck to not tip over as he moved her. She relaxed while the water beat down on the both of them. She was pissed, as she was sure he knew something, but the water felt too good. It felt like it washed away her anger the longer it touched her. And the itching she had felt since she boarded the bus was completely gone.

Whitney stared at Sam, sitting eye level with him on his lap, his broad arms wrapped around her, keeping her from falling over as the bus turned.

"We have about ten minutes before the water runs out," Sam stated, breaking their eye contact as he looked at her fin. "After that, we can't talk without the guys hearing us."

"And that would be bad?" Whitney had to jump to conclusions. Sam wasn't explaining much of anything.

"Yes, very bad," Sam replied, holding her steady with one arm and reaching forward with his other hand. He touched her fin gently, right where her knees would have been.

It was a strange and very new sensation. When she had turned into a part fish the night before, she poked and prodded the whole tail as she tried to make it go away, but having Sam touch it was so much different, a bit intimate. The ends of her tail flickered when he touched her finned knees. Sam grinned.

"Glad my new tail makes you happy, but you have a lot of explaining to do," Whitney scolded him as best she could, but she was still sitting wrapped in his arms. It was a lot less effective from that point as he protected her from every bump and turn of the road.

Sam turned back to Whitney and his smile faded. He touched the lines that randomly covered her shoulders also, and then lifted his gaze to meet hers. Her body was covered from the waist up with swirling, almost tattoo-looking lines that left her breasts covered and gave a shimmery tinge to her skin.

"I suppose the first thing I should do is show you," Sam finally responded after what seemed like forever, but couldn't have been more than ten seconds.

Every time Sam moved or touched Whitney, it felt like time was slowing down.

He wrapped his free arm back around her waist, and she could feel him move slightly beneath her. Looking down, she watched as his legs merged together and a deep blue fin appeared. Whitney didn't try to cover up her gasp. He was a mermaid also, or was that a merman? How was that possible?

Sam touched her cheek gently to get her to look back to him. Whitney was shocked a second time as his normally brown eyes were now a seafoam green-blue color.

"As you can probably guess, I'm a merperson," Sam started to explain.

"Merman?" Whitney interrupted. She really wanted to call him a mermaid, but she could tell by his serious expression it wasn't the time to kid around. Whitney felt like that a lot. When things got too serious, she couldn't help but make jokes.

"Technically I'm a siren," Sam continued like she hadn't interrupted him. "I come from a family of night humans who turn part mer in the water and sing to lure their prey to them. Night humans are people that survive on blood. Things like vampires and werewolves are true, including mermaids."

"But the mermaids are extinct. I was taught that growing up," Whitney replied. It was confusing to see a childhood fantasy of hers sitting beside her. It made her tail problem much more real.

"Taught?" Sam raised an eyebrow at her choice in words.

"I was raised as a skinwalker. We learned about the other clans in North America all the time." It wasn't like she had to hide her own night human world from Sam. He was a freaking night human after all, even if he was a very extinct night human.

Sam smiled and sighed at the same time, like he found the last piece in the puzzle.

"So that's why you turned," Sam replied. "Here I was wondering how in the world you could have a tail, but you're already a night human. It was in your DNA to be another one. I've heard of this happening in the night human world now with the new leader of the clans and all, but I didn't know it was possible for other people."

Whitney put a hand up and covered his mouth to stop him from talking. He had the wrong impression completely.

"I *was* a night human." She tried her best to emphasize the past tense of it. "A year ago I got mixed up with a witch that killed my night human side. I moved here since I'm no longer a skinwalker."

While Sam seemed like he was going to say more, he paused at her words. He stared into her eyes before suddenly looking up at the water.

"We have like two minutes left," he said quickly. "You can't tell a single person about this. The merworld is supposed to be dead. We've let everyone think that for over two hundred years. If the night human world finds out, they will come hunting us. I'll explain it all more at another time. We should meet tomorrow at lunch. Tell your friends you're taking me out to eat as payment for saving you from drowning."

"I haven't gotten paid yet," Whitney interrupted him.

"Lie to them, ask them for money, I don't care which. I need to teach you how to be a merperson or the mer will hunt you also."

Whitney opened her mouth to interrupt him again. That wasn't good enough. She needed more of an explanation. Sam covered her mouth with his hand.

"The only thing I have to tell you right now for you to survive is that all merpeople need two things. Water and blood. That's it. Your fin needs to be in the water at least once every twenty-four hours. If you go longer, you'll get itchy and dehydrated quickly. Then you'll lose control of it. Second is that we drink blood, a lot of it. It takes about ten pints of blood every four to six months. Most mer prefer to drink that all at one time, and others take a bit at a time. You'll need blood, especially now that you're new."

The water in the spout began to drizzle out. They were almost out of time.

Sam leaned closer to Whitney's ear.

"I'll teach you how to be a siren, but you can't tell a single other person about it. It would mean your death and probably mine, and not in a very nice way."

Whitney swallowed the lump in her throat. Sam sounded ominous, like he knew exactly how they would torture her to death. Maybe he did. She was already picturing the scary siren world that she was now part of. She never asked to be one, yet she was. Life was getting too complicated. Sam reached for the towel hanging on the door just out of reach of the water that had been spraying on them. Sam's legs reappeared, even though water was dripping down him still, and he moved to pick Whitney up and place her back in the seat.

Whitney grabbed his arm and moved to whisper back in his ear.

"Okay, I get it. Don't tell anyone, and I need water and blood. I get how to get the water, but what about blood?"

Back in the city where she was raised, there were blood banks night humans could just collect from. If she needed it, her friends probably could tell her where one was in every major Florida city, but since she couldn't tell anyone about being a night human, she would have no excuse for wanting blood.

Sam nodded. He hadn't thought of that, obviously. It didn't take him long to decide what to do about it though as he tilted his head to the side.

"Until I teach you how to do this safely, I'll feed you," he said quietly.

Whitney stared at him. Feed on him. She had never fed on a human in her life. Sam noticed her hesitation and took her hand, placing it on his chest. Her face turned red. The skin was smooth, yet she could feel the muscle right below the surface. She was sitting in the shower with the hot guy she had a crush on, and he was offering to feed her blood. Yep, it had to be Alternate Universe Day. It was all just too weird.

Whitney looked up into his eyes. She was a newly turned night human, and she could easily lose control. He was completely calm and not worried in the least. As she stared into his eyes, he seemed to urge her to go ahead. Whitney took a deep breath and tried to not think of what she was doing.

Waking the next morning, Whitney found that she had a text from Sam telling her where to meet him. She had no idea how he even got her number, but that wasn't the only mystery. After feeding her the night before, Sam stood up and walked out of the shower with the same shorts on that he had when came in. Whitney dried herself off and found herself back in her clothing also. How was that possible? When she had been a skinwalker, any transformation shredded her clothing. That didn't seem to be the case for the sirens.

Whitney had woken to her phone beeping from Sam's text. She would have rather slept more. After they had returned from the concert, Whitney had to walk home in the dark since Sam had to go with the guys and pretend she wasn't even there. She didn't know what time she finally fell into her bed in exhaustion. The dark never really bothered her much as she had spent most of her life as a night human. The four-mile walk was a bit much after being awake for over twenty hours and then having to sneak into her room to sleep. At least her aunt wouldn't be there in the morning. She always worked morning shifts, and sometimes afternoon and night shifts, too. She was a bit of a workaholic.

Yawning, Whitney stretched as she rolled out of bed. She needed to beg her friends for a loan before heading out to eat with Sam. After all, they had all offered to help so she wouldn't owe Sam any longer. Now she was just following through and taking them up on it. Trudy wrote her back that she could give her money, and Whitney now had one stop on her way to meet up with Sam.

She didn't want to take a shower and deal with those issues, so she just combed her hair and threw on shorts and a T-shirt over the swimsuit Sam told her to wear. Sleepiness got the best of her. She was too tired to care what she really looked like, and it didn't sound as if it mattered much since she was wearing her favorite pink polka dot bikini.

Her alarm clock began to beep, and she realized she had set it the night before, even if she didn't remember when. Picking up her phone, she checked the time since she was sure her alarm clock had to be wrong. It couldn't be that late. *Yep, it was that late.*

She ran down the stairs and out the front door, not even saying good morning to her cousin who was sitting on the couch watching TV. He said something, but she was already gone. She was going to be late unless she ran. Heck, her one stop alone, even though it was on the way, would make her late.

Crossing the next street, Whitney was half jogging. It would take her at least ten minutes to get to Trudy's house. She didn't look at the houses she passed or even the few people out walking dogs. She was on a mission to be the least amount of late as she could. More sleep would have helped, and it certainly would have made her cheerier, but what could she do? She had been out late to a rock concert. So it was kind of her own fault. When she made it there, Trudy was already waiting on the steps, money in hand like she knew that she would be running late.

Whitney smiled at her friend. That was a true friend, loaning money and waiting for her at the same time.

"I promise I'll pay you back after I get paid next Friday. I just don't want to wait any longer to start rewarding him for saving me. Otherwise, I'll have to take him out every week this summer," Whitney easily lied to her friend. She felt bad about it, but she knew the dangers of telling a day human of the night human world. She would do anything to protect her friends.

Trudy nodded along with her. "No, you don't want to owe Prince Sam. I bet he'd make you come back from college on the weekends to pay him back if you don't get it done before we leave in the fall."

Whitney couldn't help but look closer at her friend. The way they always talked about Sam made her wonder even more. It was like they knew him even though she never saw any of her friends interact with him. She was going to have to ask Sam who the sirens were in town. Could she have been friends with them all along?

"Thanks," Whitney said as she took the money. "Gotta run. I'm already late."

Trudy grinned. "Good. Make him wait. He's the one demanding you take him out, at least he could give you enough warning to plan ahead. Guys like him are so difficult."

Waving as she walked, Whitney headed off down the road in the same half walk, half jog pace she was doing before. By the time she made it to her favorite dock, she wasn't surprised to find Sam waiting. He was standing outside his Jeep. He stood almost as tall as his Jeep, and he was wearing only a sleeveless tank with his board shorts. He didn't even seem to notice as Whitney approached. His eyes were on the ocean, watching the waves while they came in. His dark, ear-length hair wasn't pulled back out of his face like it was for school normally. Instead, it flopped over his ears and around his face, keeping his eyes from Whitney.

Waves rolled onto the beach not even twenty feet from them. The sound was always soothing before to Whitney, but now it sounded almost magical, like a song was coming from the waters. She stopped, looking at her handsome date. And yes she noticed, but she was trying her best to not oogle him, or rather get caught staring. Instead, she watched the waves beside him.

"Do you hear it?" Sam finally asked after at least five minutes of standing there listening.

"The song?" Whitney asked. She hadn't visited the ocean since everything had changed. In fact, she hadn't been around any body of water since it had happened only days ago.

"Does it call to you?"

Whitney listened to the wind blow the melody closer, but she felt like she was too far away to tell. She took a step closer to see if she heard it better. Sam finally turned to her and smiled, placing a hand on her cheek to get her to face him instead of the water. His touch broke the spell the water had put on her.

"Guess it does."

Whitney had no clue what that meant, and was going to ask him before he interrupted her.

"I'm famished. Let's eat first and then go somewhere we can be alone to talk."

Whitney couldn't complain about that. She hadn't eaten breakfast either, though she wasn't exactly hungry because of missing it. Normally her stomach would be growling by eleven if she skipped a meal. She might have been thin, but it wasn't because of what she ate. She loved sweets, ate pizza once a week, and never skipped a meal for anything other than sleep.

"Hop in," he ordered her.

She turned quickly so he wouldn't catch her slight giggle that slipped out. After a year of people referring to him as Prince, she could finally see it better. She always thought he was bossy in her swim lessons because he was teaching her, but it seemed he was bossy in real life, too.

"Where are we going?" Whitney asked as Sam took a turn heading out of town.

"There's a place a bit north of here I like to get breakfast at after shows. They know me, but no one else there does, and my ... I mean, *our kind* doesn't go there. We'll get some privacy."

Our kind. That sounded strange. She had been part of the night human world, but not for the past year. She felt like she didn't belong with her aunt, or the day humans around her, but she didn't feel like she belonged home with her brother and the skinwalkers. It was kind of nice to hear she was part of something again.

Whitney nodded to Sam since it seemed like he was waiting for a reaction of his choice of places. It was all so secretive, and a bit strange for her. Where she lived and grew up, everyone seemed to know about the skinwalkers. The people in her town were either a night human or married to one. There were no secrets beyond her friend, who everyone had kept in the dark because they didn't know who her father was. Whitney never had to worry about talking to her other best friend, Owen, as they walked around town. No one worried about it.

Sam drove in silence while Whitney wondered what he was thinking about. His eyes were fixed on the road, even as hers drifted to the ocean when it peeked out every now and then through the houses they passed. She didn't understand what he meant initially, saying it called to him, but she did now. It didn't matter where she was looking or how many houses were in the way; she knew exactly where the ocean was. She wondered why it was like that, and couldn't wait to finally get some answers.

CHAPTER 4

Sam just stared at Whitney as she perused the menu. This was his normal Saturday morning breakfast joint, so he already knew what he was going to order: two eggs over easy, two sausage, two bacon, two biscuits, and two pancakes. Maybe it was a bit much, but he was really hungry. He needed blood but he also needed food, in large quantities some times.

"So ..." Whitney began as she finally set down her menu.

"No talk about last night or anything to do with last night," Sam quickly told her.

It wasn't a safe place to talk about either of those things. He had to keep the siren secret, and chose to keep the music secret also. It was like he had a few other lives he lived, but it was better that way. Keeping them separate kept him from ever letting out secrets, and his life was full of them.

Whitney huffed a little, and he had to hide his smile. He liked her little huffs. She tended to do them when she was frustrated, but not mad. When she was mad, she was more likely to just tell you what she thought. Huffs meant she was only a little mad. And it was cute to watch her cheeks puff and her loose hair fly out of her eyes.

"Then what would you like to talk about?" she finally asked.

Sam grinned. "Well, how about you tell me more about you," he suggested.

He had done his homework as much as he could about her, but there was very little to go on. When he first saw her, he wanted to know everything he could about her. Digging into her past proved very unfruitful, and he had to just listen to her talk to friends to learn more. On paper, there was very little to go on. Obviously, he didn't know she had been a former night human. Heck, he didn't even know it was possible to take that out of someone.

"Um, like what?" Whitney seemed genuinely embarrassed being asked to talk about herself. Her cheeks got a little rosy color to them. Sam was content to just watch her and let her squirm, but the waitress took that exact moment to show up.

"Hey, Sam," the cute brunette said as she moseyed up to the table, making sure that her uniform skirt puffed against the table top. "I didn't know Mark had a sister."

Sam looked up at her and smiled as nicely as he could. You never wanted to tick off your server at a restaurant. Lydia was always hitting on him, but he did his best to deflect her advances. Mark had already taken her on a couple dates and fed off her. It was kind of the code amongst the siren not to feed on the same person someone else had. Whatever the reason, Mark hadn't called her back in the past couple months. Without knowing the why, Sam knew exactly when Mark stopped calling Lydia as she then made passing remarks to him about everything.

"Nope, not his sister, she's my new *friend*," Sam said, making Whitney's cheeks turn a brighter shade of red when he said friend, making it sound like much more. It wasn't anything more than that, but a guy could dream. That never hurt anything.

"Oh." Lydia seemed genuinely disappointed. She pulled out her pad of paper and pen and immediately cheered up as she thought. "What about the other guy you bring with you sometimes? I forget his name. The quiet one. Does he have a *friend*?" She used the same emphasis.

"I'm not sure at the moment," Sam cryptically replied. He knew perfectly well that Leo had a girlfriend. They were almost essentially married, or close enough. Both of them were excited to graduate from high school and head back to the island, but he didn't need to tell Lydia that.

"Well, next time bring him with," Lydia ordered Sam, tapping her pencil on the pad of paper and smiling as she thought, probably about Leo. At least she was off him for the moment. "So what'll it be?"

"Two Much Special for me," Sam answered, giving Whitney a bit more time to decide, which he was sure she hadn't done yet. "And a large orange juice."

"Of course," Lydia replied back. "Over easy?"

"Yes, please."

"And you, *friend*?" Lydia turned to Whitney. The term *friend* sounded a bit sourer this time as she said it. Even though he had deflected her to thinking about Leo, she wasn't too happy with Whitney.

"Cinnamon pancakes and a cup of coffee," she replied.

Lydia nodded and walked away, not trying to get her to order more. Sam knew girls as he had several sisters. They were easy to make jealous, and fought often. He turned his complete attention to Whitney. She wasn't like all the girls he knew.

"Coffee?" Sam asked. "Really? You like that stuff? Doesn't it stunt your growth?"

"I don't think it hurt me much. Actually, I'm glad I'm not six foot four." Whitney shrugged as he still looked like he couldn't believe she liked coffee. "And I was out really late last night. Someone kept me out way past my bedtime to get all my beauty sleep. I'll need it to stay awake all day, and yes, I like that stuff. You should try it some time. I bet it would help in your lifestyle."

Sam grinned. He had said no talking, and with anyone else, they would have never even tried to mention the night before; but not Whitney. Try as he might to get her to do something, she was like a current in the water that was going to do as it pleased, no matter what was passing through. Sam liked that about her.

"What do you want to know?" Whitney asked, turning back to his original question. That was also new for Sam.

Ask any siren to talk about themselves and they could write you a novel, maybe even a five book series, but not with Whitney. She never talked about herself.

"Anything, really. I know that you came here a year ago and that you had to move. You live with your aunt and cousin, and you work at Bingos. I also know you swim better than most of the people I've ever taught to swim, which I like to think is because I'm a great teacher, and now I know that you like to drink coffee." Sam listed everything, but basically was saying he didn't know much.

Whitney shrugged. "That pretty much sums me up." Infuriatingly cute, she didn't add more.

"I highly doubt it."

Lydia came back and set their drinks on the table along with a glass of water for each of them. Turning to leave, she knocked into Whitney's glass, spilling the water across the table and onto Whitney's lap. Whitney gasped, not at the cold, but because water just got on her. Sam concentrated and kept the water on top of her shorts, not allowing it to seep into them. She was afraid of turning, and he should have been afraid for her, but he could protect her. She was a siren now, and it was a duty he was all too happy to do.

"Oh, no. I'm sorry about that," Lydia said as she reached down and patted Whitney's lap with the extra paper towels in her work skirt. "I'll go get you more towels."

Whitney let out her breath as her legs stayed legs instead of a fin.

"Why in the world?" she asked as she looked up at Sam, finally noticing the water hadn't gone through her shorts.

He nodded and waved his hand a little to make the rest of the water pooling on her shorts and shirt move to the table.

"You can—"

Lydia came back and interrupted Whitney. She handed them more paper towels and took the soaked ones away.

"What did I say about no talking about last night?" Sam replied with a smile.

He was never going to get her to stop asking questions. The food needed to come quickly as he was sure it was going to take everything to divert her attention to the land world instead of asking questions that could get them both in trouble if the wrong person overheard. She was a challenge, but one he more than ready to accept.

The meal was finished, and Whitney was glad to be leaving. The food was great for being a little hole-in-the-wall diner, but the service was a bit lacking. From the puppy-dog eyes the waitress was giving him, she was more than a little in love with Sam, even if he didn't seem to notice. The waitress hadn't stopped staring the whole time, and it was more than a little nerve-wracking to eat while the girl stared at them. Whitney had a distinct feeling the knocked-over water was on purpose also and that was just dangerous for her new self.

As they left after paying less than she expected, Sam led them away from the diner, but not toward his car. Whitney would have asked, but with her new siren senses, she knew where the little path would lead. She could already feel the ocean calling.

"Come here often?" Whitney joked at the pathway.

He didn't look over his shoulder to give her a reply.

The song grew louder as they walked closer. It was like she had radar for the ocean and could estimate that it was only going to take two more minutes to walk there. Whitney paused as they stepped out of the trees and tall grasses onto a sandy beach. One would have never known from the diner that the beach and ocean were behind there, unless you were Sam, of course.

"This is where we go to get privacy?" Whitney looked down the beach. It actually connected up with a longer beach that went around a bend, but no one was around. It was perfectly empty and very perfect in her eyes.

"Nope. I got a better plan for that."

Sam pulled off his shirt and stepped into the water. Whitney could feel the call of the ocean, but she still had enough sense to stay out of the water if she didn't want to instantly turn into a half-fish. Previously being a night human might have helped with her sense of control.

"Talking in the water sounds great except for one problem," Whitney said as she watched Sam wade knee deep in the water. "Can we talk underwater?"

Whitney really had no clue, but seeing that she didn't know if anyone else was near the beach or just around the bend, she figured it was a good idea to stay out of the water.

"Leave your stuff here with my stuff," Sam directed her.

Whitney raised an eyebrow. She was getting the common theme. Sam liked to be in charge. A please would have been nice, but then again, she wasn't sure she ever heard him say that.

"No one comes this far down the beach. It's safe to leave everything, probably safe to talk, but I like to be extra sure," he explained. Still not a please, but it would do. She liked explanations as much as courtesy.

Whitney slipped off her shirt and shorts, but still didn't go into the water. Standing on the edge, she watched the waves lap the shore near her toes. It was tempting to just stick a toe in, but she had more control than that.

Sam jogged out of the water and scooped her into his dry arms all in one motion before she could complain.

"I forget how new this is to you. Sorry about that," Sam apologized while basically explaining nothing. "I've been this way my whole life and don't remember what it's like to begin with."

Whitney normally would have had a witty comeback or some snarky comment to go with his admission, but she was pressed close against him, so she was a little distracted. It had felt so different when Sam had touched her fin the day before. Now she realized it wasn't just his touch on her fin, but his touch in general. Her heart picked up its beating, and she tried not to look him in the eyes, which would place her lips just inches from him. No way was she supposed to fall for the guy that turned her into a mermaid. No way.

Sam carried Whitney over to the large stones sticking out of the water—they reached for at least ten or fifteen feet into the air and stretched farther into the ocean—and set her on a ledge that kept her out of the water.

"At low tide, people like to come down to these rocks and walk around them, but at high tide, everyone stays away," Sam explained. "There are pockets between the rocks that people can get trapped in, so it isn't safe."

The rock formations were beautiful and perfect to stand on. There was a ledge that was more than eight inches wide, wide enough not just for Whitney but also Sam's feet to stand. Whitney stared at the porous gray stone that shot up into the sky. There were even ledges that allowed her to hold on to it. She turned to Sam in the water, and his hand was still on her back, steadying her. He was waiting for her to say she was fine before he let go. Bossy but a gentleman.

Whitney nodded, hanging on to the stone as Sam jumped up beside her. He walked his way down the ledge, going more than thirty feet into the ocean. Blue-green water sloshed below her, and it was exhilarating. Old new-to-swimming Whitney would have been terrified, but now, the water didn't scare her at all. It was actually very inviting. Sam led the way to the tip of the rocks and around a corner, keeping them from the view of anyone who might possibly see them from the beach.

Sitting down carefully on the ledge, Sam let his feet dip into the water. He kicked it a little with his toes and not a fin.

"How do you do that?" Whitney finally asked, hoping he would answer instead of evade her questions as he had all morning.

"Not too hard, really." He held his hands up in defense. "We learn when we're younger. Takes maybe a week or two to perfect. Don't worry. You don't have to be afraid of water all the time when you're around people. You'll learn quickly; I don't doubt. You have a knack for learning things quicker than a normal person."

With her cheeks turning red a bit at his compliment, Whitney nodded but didn't sit beside him. Sam grinned up at her and slid forward, plopping into the ocean feet first. From her vantage point, Whitney watched him bob down and come back up to break the surface.

"Are you coming?" he asked, grinning at her.

Second thoughts began to drift into her mind. Yes, she could swim, and with Sam around she was safe. She never felt otherwise with him. He had saved her from drowning half a dozen times, but still she hesitated. It was the ocean, and the water was deep enough she couldn't see the bottom. And there was the one detail of swimming with her legs was one thing, but she'd have to swim with a fin now. She had a very good feeling it would be different.

"What about someone seeing us from out there?" Whitney made up a lame excuse, and she knew from Sam's face he didn't buy it.

"No one is around for miles. I'd know if they were. Heck, once you get in the water, you'd be able to tell, too. It's like built-in sonar or something. Now quit stalling, scaredy-cat, before I climb back up and push you in."

A pout formed on her lips as she glared at him. She hated that he thought she was scared. She wasn't. It was more the technicalities she was thinking about. Placing one hand on her hip while still holding on to the wall, she planned to give him a piece of her mind before jumping in. That thought was lost when something crawled over her hand. She let go of the rock, dropping right into the ocean, mouth open and all.

Whitney moved to bob back up to the surface and yell at Sam more, but she couldn't find it in her to do so. From above, the ocean looked like a vast scary place, but below the water, it was warm and inviting. Plants grew around her, and fish swam between them in her aqua blue paradise. Whitney didn't think about how to swim with a fin. It just moved like she wanted while she made a circle around toward the large, now dark-brown-looking rocks that shot straight out of the ocean floor. When she made it almost all the way around, she found Sam underwater with her as she eagerly took in the world around her. He moved closer, his blue tail flicking to keep him right next to her.

Opening her mouth to ask what was next, she realized she couldn't talk underwater. Sam grinned more and seemed to give off the sensation of laughing. He reached forward and took her hand, tugging her closer to him and pulling her off her balance. It felt like she had tripped and ended up in his arms on land, but much slower and softer in the buoyant water.

'No talking,' Sam mouthed to her.

Yep, she got that memo already.

Whitney looked closer at him in the water. His sun-kissed, tanned chest now had more lines around him, making what she always thought was four tattoos on his upper arm really more pronounced. They almost seemed to shimmer like the various lines that ran up his chest also. She stopped checking him out when she got to his neck. Slits were lined up vertically above his collar bone.

'What are those?' Whitney mouthed and pointed to them.

Sam didn't answer, but instead backed up a little, allowing her to regain her balance. Then he tugged on her hand to move forward. It felt strange to swim without kicking, but at least her fin knew what it was doing. Sam pulled her down deeper into the water toward the bottom of the stone structures. As they descended into the darker water, she expected to see less, but instead, she actually saw clearer. Sam was aiming for a hole in the rocks ahead.

Whitney held on as he led them into the stone structure and around a pathway he was obviously familiar with. She looked around in awe as the stone was much more than just a dirty brown blob. She could make out plants that lived on it. Down below where she saw sand, she could make out creatures walking around. She was going to have to get back home and look it all up. Seeing this new world, she wanted to know about everything she saw. Before she got the chance to see much more, Sam was pulling her up through an opening that led to the surface, as it was much brighter that direction.

They got to the surface, and Whitney automatically gasped for air even though she didn't need it. She should have needed it. They had been under at least five minutes straight, or even longer.

The filtered light came down to leave shadows all over the rock walls surrounding them. There was a small hole at least twenty feet above them in the rocks, and a shoreline not even ten feet away now. Around them, they were completely surrounded by the stone she had been climbing on. There were very few plants and just as few animals in the little cove they had come to. It was more than quiet, almost silent. Only the lapping of the water on the shore and them breaking the surface of the water made any noise at all. It was completely serene and peaceful in Sam's little hiding spot.

"Gills," Sam said as he pulled her toward the shore. She didn't think they had swam all the way back to the edge of the ocean, but they must have been going that direction the whole time they twisted and turned through the underwater tunnels.

"Gills?"

"Those lines on my neck and yours, too, once you go underwater."

Whitney immediately felt for her neck to see if she had the same flaps of skin. It tickled to touch them, and she almost laughed. She had gills. Now that wasn't something that happened every day.

"Gills?" she repeated. That explained why she didn't

need to catch her breath on their underwater adventure.

"Yes. Now I don't have to worry about you drowning in swimming lessons. You can go back and forth as much as you want while doing laps and never have to surface." Sam grinned at her, and she playfully punched him in the arm for teasing her.

Sam pulled Whitney forward enough so they could sit on the sandy bottom of the hidden cove they were in now, but still have their lower halves, including their fins, covered.

"We have at least one hour before we have to make it back," Sam told her. "The water is on its way out, and people can actually see in here after that. They wouldn't be able to get to us, but part of being a siren is keeping everything about us a secret."

One hour wasn't nearly enough time to talk.

"And I need half of that to explain more of the mer world to you," Sam added.

Whitney's face soured. It was going to take forever to learn anything at this rate.

"And just so that you don't waste any of your time asking questions about stuff I planned to tell you, I'll go first," he explained while nodding. Whether it had been to Whitney or himself, she couldn't tell.

Whitney couldn't help the pout that formed. She had hundreds of questions floating around in her mind, and not enough time to get answers. It would have been easier if being a siren came with an instruction manual. Okay, it wasn't that bad that her instruction manual had beautiful eyes and a rock-hard body. It was a pretty good trade off, but would be better if she had unlimited access to his answers, too. He was close to perfect, just not quite perfect enough to pull it off teaching her everything she needed to know in thirty minutes. Who knew, though? Sam seemed to be full of surprises lately.

Whitney listened as Sam talked on and on about the mer and siren in general. She knew some of the stuff, and the other was new, yet boring. He told about the night human wars and how all the mer sided with the wrong side, how the sirens helped but didn't really care who won, and how they escaped being found by building their own island world to live at away from everyone else. It was a cool story, but it didn't help her in the basics of how to survive as a mermaid. So far all she knew was that it was close to impossible to turn someone into a mer, and even telling non-mer about them would get them exiled. Neither of those two things helped her much.

She was more than ready with questions when Sam took a breath and looked at her, trying to see if she understood his last lengthy explanation about why the mer were secret. Whitney understood secrets even if night humans weren't secret to her growing up. Her best friend was forbidden by her uncle to learn about night humans. Whitney was a good friend and night human, so she never told her friend about it without permission.

"Okay," Whitney drew out her reply. "So keep it a secret. I'm willing to do that. I don't even want to find out what sunning as a torture method means." That was one point which had caught her attention. Sam had mentioned it more than once.

"No, you don't."

"Then how about we get to the stuff I really need to know about."

Sam looked like he was lost. To him, what he had been explaining was what she needed to know. Whitney tried not to giggle at his confused face. It didn't take more than a couple sentences to understand that Sam was proud of being a siren.

Whitney had done her best to listen as much as she could, but she had been raised to protect day humans. When he talked easily about draining the blood of drowning day humans to feed, she knew she could never truly understand him. He made it sound like it was fine to kill them since they were dying already, but every fiber in her body said dying or not, you had to try and save them. It had been a fun fleeting thought of being part of the night human world again, but it was just that, fleeting. Her best course of action would be to keep herself a secret and continue her life without the sirens.

"So last night you said we need water and blood to survive. Is that all?"

Realization set in on Sam's face. He hadn't spoken a single thing about actually living as a siren.

"Yes. Basically, that's all you need."

"Then I can live anywhere, right? You said all merpeople live near oceans. Is there a reason for that?" Whitney proved she had been listening, at least kind of.

"Yes, all you need is blood and water, but you don't want to stray too far on land. If for some reason you don't get to water within twenty-four hours you become itchy. After forty-eight hours you become dehydrated. Even if you're drinking water, you'll still feel thirsty and your skin itches like crazy. It's not like a day human who gets lost and goes without water. You won't just die; you'll die very slowly, and you'll feel like you're drying out the whole time. You'll lose energy to move and try to find water, but death will take weeks if not months. You'll suffer like that, unable to move, with your body feeling like you can't itch it enough, while you dream of water."

Okay, that sounded horrible.

"Got it. Stay near water," Whitney replied. "Does it have to be ocean water, or can a lake or river work?" She needed details. That's what she met up with him for.

"Rivers and lakes are fine, but I don't know more specifics about them. Being that you want to stay a secret, mer really don't travel far inland. Out in the ocean if someone sees a siren, most of the time they just assume they see a mirage. The ocean is huge, and no one actually has seen a mermaid up close. In a river or lake, they'd know what they're looking at."

That made sense. On to the next question.

"And blood. How do you feed? Who do you feed on?"

This was a good point and one that Whitney needed to learn. As a skinwalker, she could go to any blood bank and ask for a pint of blood. With mermaids having to remain a secret since they shouldn't exist in the night human world, that made getting blood there a no-go. And she wasn't about to start killing day humans.

Sam laid back in the water, letting his body float to the surface, and his blue fin flicked a little bit. The motion of his tail made her smile. It was hard to tell with his sun-kissed skin, but Whitney thought his cheeks might have been a bit redder.

"We're siren," he began. Whitney didn't lean back to join him. She really needed to figure this one out. If she needed blood to survive, she had to know how to go about getting it. It wasn't like she could feed on Sam for the rest of her life.

"And ..."

"We can put people into a trance by singing so that we can lure them into the water and feed on them." Sam floated next to her but didn't look up.

"And ..." There was more, Whitney could tell.

Sighing, he finally sat up. He wasn't fooling Whitney with such a simple answer.

"I teach swim lessons to feed on people. Normally a siren will find a drowning person, or lure someone into the water to kill them. One human can last months. It's simple that way. I prefer not to draw any notice to us on land, and forbid the siren I take care of from doing that. We feed only a pint or two on several humans at least once a week instead."

That was a lot of blood. Whitney now wondered how many dead day humans were out there because they were lured off to the sea.

"And you can't just come clean to the night humans and

use donated blood?" Whitney knew this was impossible. Sam had explained what she already knew. The sirens were on the losing side of the night human wars. They weren't supposed to exist, and if they came out of hiding, they would be killed for it.

"That's what I was explaining before. Sirens are forbidden. It's death on sight for us. Any siren found, whether they're two or seventy, are sentenced to death by the governing night humans, and they are free game for hunters."

Whitney stared at him in shock. She had heard of hunters growing up. They were abnormally strong day humans who felt it was their duty to rid the world of bad night humans. They were given leeway to hunt those the night human councils deemed dangerous, but that was all she knew about them. Skinwalkers weren't dangerous to day humans. Whitney had never been on that side before. It was strange to find herself sitting where she was. Even worse was to find out just being a siren made her a "bad guy."

"That's why I don't let the sirens kill around here. It keeps us free of hunters." Sam seemed more confident in his admission of how he fed.

"I just sing a little and then I can feed on anyone I want?" Whitney asked. She needed more details, especially on something so essential to her life again.

"Oh no," Sam quickly replied. "You'd do best to not sing at all until you've had lots of practice controlling it. Singing the wrong thing could lead to you accidentally drowning someone. Or, you might put them in a trance permanently. Singing is something you'll need lots of practice at before you try it on a day human. And even then you'd have to be careful to not drain them when you feed. You'll have to have complete control of your night human side. Siren instinct is to kill. To just drink is something you have to practice at."

Whitney flapped her arms in exasperation. She didn't want to kill or hurt anyone, but she couldn't go get blood the normal way. What was she supposed to do?

Sam caught on easily to her frustration.

"So … what? Do I just feed on fish until then?" That must have been why fish didn't repulse her now. She was one of them.

Sam laughed. "No one feeds on fish. Fish are cold-blooded animals. We have to feed on warm blooded animals, like mammals, and I don't think you'd find a mer that was willing to eat anything but human blood."

Whitney threw her arms up in the air. He was making it impossible for her. What was she supposed to do?

"Until I can teach you how to control your siren singing and feeding, I'll feed you. We probably should do that now before we head back."

Back? Whitney didn't get an ounce of her questions answered.

"Don't worry. You owe me several meals, so we can come back here tomorrow, too." Sam seemed to understand her frustration.

He pushed off from where he was sitting and swam under into the deeper water. Whitney followed and bumped into him when he stopped, positioning himself upright. Steadying her, Sam pulled her up to eye level with him. Her head broke the surface, and she sucked in her breath as she floated close to him. Sam pulled her closer.

Sam was beautiful as a day human, but as a mer he was exquisite. His dark hair was now slicked back and almost black in color. His upper body was lean but muscular in all the right places, including abs that any bodybuilder would have died to have. Lines swirled up his body, marking his normal tattoos to make more of a bold statement. All his music fans would have died from a heart attack if they could see him as a siren. She didn't know rock star Sam could get any hotter. Whitney's heart beat fast as he held her close.

Sam raised an eyebrow as if to say he saw her staring at him.

"Umm, what do I do?" Whitney asked, stalling and hoping he thought her hesitation was from confusion, and not from checking him out.

Sam grinned. "You didn't seem to have a problem feeding last night. Maybe I'm not holding you close enough."

Sam's arms tightened around, pressing his body to hers as her cheeks burned red. She was positive he saw, but instead of teasing her more, he tilted his head, exposing the vein in his neck. As embarrassing as it was to be held close, it was what made it all easier. Whitney didn't think and just let her body move on its own as she bit down.

CHAPTER 5

Sam balanced on the rocks behind Whitney as she made her way back to the cove from the day before. Confidently she climbed around the rocks until she got to the edge where they needed to go under. She didn't wait for him to catch up as she stepped forward and fell into the water. Sam waited for a second for her to surface before he realized she was already heading toward the opening to the tunnels underneath the rock. He dove in behind her and caught up as she made the first turn correctly.

Initially, he had been worried about how she would adjust, but he should have known better. Whitney was nothing like any day human he'd ever met. She was special. There wasn't a single thing to worry about. She was a natural.

She turned again and kept going forward without looking back to see if he was following. Not just special and confident, but also smart. Sam wanted to show her the merworld she was now part of, but was secretly happy she couldn't fully join the sirens. If any of the other males found her, he would have to fight to be her mate. For now, she was just his and his alone.

Whitney made it to the cove perfectly, but didn't go farther up the sand bank to sit down.

"Okay, I listened to your stories yesterday, and while informative, they didn't help me with anything. If you want me to survive as a siren, I need to learn how to actually survive. Like, how do I actually do stuff?"

Her hands were on her hips as she lectured him. Amazingly, her tail kept her perfectly straight up and down. It took most sirens years to be able to float without using their arms for balance. Not Whitney.

"Fine," he replied, and she looked confused, as if she was ready for a fight that wasn't coming. He liked being able to throw her off balance even though he couldn't do it physically, because she was good at being a siren. "What do you want to start with?"

"Um." Her confidence was temporarily gone. "I need to learn how you keep legs around water. That would be a good place to start." The latter sounded like it was more to herself than him.

"True, that would be helpful." Sam moved past her to the shallow water and walked up on the sand before sitting down. It was a bit teasing to do so, but then again, it also felt like showing off. A large part of him wanted to show off and get her attention. He wanted her to like him as much as he was falling for her.

"Yes, just like that," Whitney said as she watched him from the deeper water. "How do you do it?" She swam only a little closer but kept deep enough to be able to swim around.

"I just tell my fin to go away and that I need legs," Sam replied. It really was that easy once you could do it.

Whitney scrunched up her face. She looked like she was trying. He liked that expression. Who was he kidding? He liked all of her expressions.

"And?" she prompted him.

"And that's it. You've been a mer for less than a week. I don't think that side of you is really ready to listen to your inner self-telling it to go away. Didn't you used to be part cat?"

Whitney seemed to try again; then she gave up before swimming closer to sit in the shallow water beside him rather than shout across the ten feet between them.

"Yes."

"When you were in your human form, could you still feel the cat inside of you?"

She seemed to ponder that. By the looks of it, she never considered that her cat was a part of her, so that explanation wasn't going to work.

"Okay. Guess not," Sam replied before she could. He could read the answer on her face. "The best way I can explain it is that the siren side you see is a part of me, and the human side is the other part. When I transform, I'm both at the same time, and when I'm just human, it is still there. The siren is still beneath the surface. You can use your singing to lure people whether you have a tail or not, just like you can tell your tail to go away."

"And what if it doesn't work like that for me? I'm not exactly the same kind as you," Whitney said as she bit her lip. Sam tried not to look at her lips. He was using all the self-control he had to not try to kiss her as it was.

"I'm sure it will work the same for you, but you might have to wait a little bit. It normally can take weeks before the two sides of you settle into a familiar place. The best way I can describe it is that you have two different halves to you—your day human side and your mer side. When one is there, the other isn't. The mer side is so new that you can't control it. It will get better. I promise."

His words seemed to have a good effect; she had stopped biting her lip, at least for the moment. He wasn't that sure what else she was going to want to know about, or if he could even teach her. Being a siren was just part of who he was. It was strange to have to think about everything and explain it. But then again, it was fun. He had never met anyone like Whitney, and he was going to do his best to make sure she survived the merworld he had accidentally put her in.

Lying back in the shallow water, Whitney let the water bounce her up to the surface. She bobbed around a bit as she thought. She tried her best to imagine her legs, but there was still a fin. She didn't need to look down to know that; she could feel it. After a few minutes, Whitney gave up and sat back up. She would have to spend time at home in the bath trying to will her fin to go away when it was wet. Maybe she would have more luck while alone than being watched, and she was being watched. Sam hadn't taken his eyes off her since they entered the cove. Besides, she needed to use the private time with Sam now to ask all of her questions.

"So yesterday ..." she began. Sam was watching her still. She saw something in his eyes when he looked at her, but she wasn't sure what it meant. "When the waitress spilled the drink on me, how come it didn't soak into my clothes?"

Luckily, they had a different server at the restaurant today. Whitney was relieved. The other one made her nervous, like "plotting behind her back on how to get rid of her" nervous. Whitney had dealt with her share of girls that didn't want her to be friends with the guy they liked. It was always strange to her because all the guys back home weren't allowed to date her. Skinwalkers had to date day humans, and since she was one of the only female skinwalkers, it meant no dates from the guys she was really just friends with. That didn't stop all the other girls, though. Whitney had learned to ignore it, but a waitress accidentally spilling water on her was a bit more dangerous these days. She was glad that Sam had some tricks to save her from going all fishy.

"Oh, you noticed that?" he asked innocently.

"Um, yeah. I didn't sprout a fish tail in the restaurant, so yep. I noticed that."

Sam shrugged. "Being part of the sea makes us able to control the motion of water when on land."

"So, in other words, you can go inland and just summon water to you?" It was confusing to Whitney, and she needed to understand it better. She wasn't looking for an excuse to live away from the ocean. She didn't want to be trapped, but she was pretty sure she could never leave it now.

"No, we can't summon it. We can control it, manipulate it."

Sam demonstrated as he pointed to the water in front of him, which moved up just as he directed it with his finger. Soon it was standing straight in the air. Whitney leaned forward and touched the water. It was still wet, but just standing there. Her hand breaking through it didn't make it move back to the ground like she expected.

"Cool. Can you teach me?"

"Not until you find the balance between your siren and human side."

Whitney pouted. All this Zen talk wasn't fair. She was being thrown into the siren world, where she was expected to hide, not just from day humans but the siren also, and she could do basically nothing. It was like she would be better off becoming a hermit in a cave the way Sam told it. If she did that, at least then she might go all perfect with her siren side like he talked about.

"Fine. Then what can you teach me?"

"Can I continue from yesterday?" Sam asked. He was serious.

"Um, no. That stuff, while great, doesn't help me. I can't be part of your merworld, so as much as it's an interesting story, I need more real world stuff. Like what about the mer at school? How many are there? Who are they? How do I avoid them?"

Sam nodded at her questions like he hadn't thought of them.

"I suppose that's fair. There are just over three hundred sirens at our schools. Most of them are at the high school with a few in the junior high. All of the teenage sirens come to land to learn a bit before going back. We don't have schools on the island."

Whitney's mouth dropped open. She was expecting something like twenty or thirty. Not three hundred. She began to count in her head. There were five hundred students in each grade, making the high school just about two thousand students. Three hundred of those students were mermaids. Unbelievable.

"Okay. Now I'm not sure if you can give me all those names, and I'll remember them." Three hundred was beyond what anyone could remember. She wasn't certain she knew the names of three hundred students in the school.

"Well, it's easier than that. All the people I hang out with are sirens. All the people you hang out with are also. And anyone you catch calling me Prince Sam is a siren, too."

Whitney felt the blush creep up her cheeks. She didn't know he had heard them call him that. Her friends were all sirens. That was something she needed to ponder a bit.

"Wait a second," she said as the blush went away. "If my friends are all sirens, and so are yours, why aren't they all friends?"

Sam laughed. "How do you know we aren't all friends?"

"Because I've heard my friends talk about you and your friends all the time. I know they don't like you guys."

Sam laughed again. "No, I'd expect they don't like us much. My father is an idiot thinking that if the blues and greens can just live peacefully on land together something will change. Nothing is ever going to change there."

"Blues and greens?" Now he was back to confusing talk.

"Did you listen to anything I told you yesterday?"

"Um, yeah?" That was the answer he wanted, hopefully.

"The siren world is divided into blues and greens. It's decided by the color of your fin. If you're a blue, you stay with the blues, and if you're a green, you are with the greens. I happen to be a blue." Sam flicked his tail out of the water. It was more of an inky blue color now in the dark cove. There was only a bit of sunlight peeking through the clouds.

"And that means ..." Whitney prompted him to continue. She didn't need to get distracted from her goal of getting answers.

"That I'm part of the upper layer of the siren world.

Okay, you weren't listening. What you need to know, all summed up, is that there are tons of hierarchies in the mer world. Overall the half-human merpeople have a ranking. Siren sit right at the top of types of mer. We're stronger than all the groups, and with our singing, we have control that none of the others have over humans. But not all sirens have total control. Only blues can control both day and night humans with their voice. We have a division in the sirens of blue and green. Their tail tells us which kind they are before they even sing."

"Um." Whitney glanced down at her own pink tail. "Then I'm not a siren?"

Sam looked down and watched her tail flick in the water. Smiling, he shook his head. "No. I'm sure you are a siren, but I have no idea why your tail is pink."

"I kind of thought it had to do with the fact that I wear pink all the time. The first time I transformed with clothing on, I was wearing pink. It isn't because you always wear blue that you have a blue fin?" Whitney already knew the answer.

"That's a good theory, but no. You can wear any color clothing you want, and it doesn't affect your fin color."

Whitney shrugged. "It was worth a shot. I had to figure out some reason you don't lose your clothing when you turn. That still baffles me beyond anything. Night humans I get, but transforming fully clothed and returning to that clothing afterward? I just don't get it."

Sam laughed. "You can understand turning half fish, but not your clothes disappearing? Isn't it a bit magical in the first place, being able to turn into a mermaid? Why can't there be other magic involved?"

Okay, he had a point there.

"Like your magical eyes?"

Sam grinned. "So glad you noticed. At least you pay attention to part of me."

"Um, yeah. And I've noticed before."

"Dang. I thought I kept them hidden. Yes, my eyes change color when my siren side comes out. It doesn't mean I'm going to transform, just that there's more of that side taking control. It happens when you get emotional." Sam smiled sheepishly. "We shouldn't let our siren sides do that, but it's hard to always be in control."

"When you were mad at your brother in the lunchroom the other day, your siren side came out?" She had no clue what that meant.

Sam shrugged as he ran his hands through his drying hair.

"My siren side is more powerful than my human one. When I feel any sort of emotion strongly, it tends to leak out. Most blues have everything all under control. But then again, most blues don't feel any emotion very strongly. Sirens overall are very selfish beings, but blues are by far the worst. I don't want you caught by the sirens because I know they won't give you a chance. Your pink fin means you don't fit into their perfect society view of all things. And they don't want that. Everything has to line up just right. It's actually rather boring. And if you don't fit perfectly into siren order, it's like you don't belong, and they make sure you feel that every waking moment."

Sounded like personal experience to Whitney.

"And your brother?"

"Is as blue as you can get. And is a royal pain. He's into everything that will bring him higher on the blue power list, and trust me, he doesn't have too much farther to go to be on top. I hope if that ever happens, someone will just put me out of my misery. He's not a good person. Please promise me to never talk to him or make eye contact with him if he decides to stop by school again. The guy is bad news."

Sam looked sad, but not at his words, more like he didn't exactly like his family. Whitney couldn't imagine being related to someone you hated. Her little brother was a pain growing up, but he was still her little brother.

"It sounds like you have a great family," Whitney added

sarcastically.

"Oh, they're just the best. That's why I volunteered to come to land and watch over everyone by the time I was fourteen. I couldn't leave fast enough. They are all like Tim. And I had to put up with him here on land until he graduated. I was happy he left. Now if he could just stay away like everyone else."

"They? How many siblings do you have?"

"I have fifteen brothers and ten sisters, and I had three older brothers that are now dead."

Whitney stared at Sam as he lay back in the water and floated, gazing up at the open sky peeking out from between the rock cracks. His family was huge, and her shock didn't seem to register with him. All she had was one little brother.

"Wow. Your parents sound like busy people," Whitney remarked as she lay back also.

Sam laughed again, but it wasn't a happy laugh this time.

"Not my parents. My father. He likes to keep the sirens populated with blues. Did you know it's actually a law that all blue couples must have at least six children? My dad, the overachiever, decided he wanted at least twenty-five. Lucky me to be the last of all of them."

There was no love in his voice when Sam spoke of his family. Whitney felt a little bad for him. Her little brother would always be part of her life, and even now she looked at her younger cousin just like a brother. She loved them both and would do anything for them. She had a feeling Sam didn't feel that way about his siblings.

"What were you and Tim fighting about?" Whitney was curious. It sounded so serious back in the cafeteria. Heck, they sounded like they were threatening each other for a bit.

"My birthday." He pushed himself under the water. Whitney had to wait for him to resurface to find out more. Sam came back up with his hair slicked back in place.

"You were arguing about your birthday?" Okay, that did sound as odd as she thought it would.

Sighing, he scooted back farther to lie with his head on the sandy beach, his body still in the water. Whitney took that as the direction for her to go also. He didn't seem excited about his birthday, and there had to be a story behind it. More siren mysteries to solve if only he would tell her about it.

"Okay, since we covered you weren't listening really well yesterday, I'm just going to go ahead and repeat things I told you."

Whitney was glad he couldn't see the blush creep back to her cheeks.

"Birthdays are a big deal in the siren world. We typically have celebrations that have hundreds of people at each of them."

Whitney didn't know hundreds of people to invite to a birthday celebration. Then again, his family was huge all on its own.

"Certain birthdays are marked as extra special and eighteen is one of them." Sam continued, yet stopped again. He seemed to get caught up in his thoughts.

"What about other ages?" Whitney asked, sensing his hesitation.

"Well, there's your coming of age birthday party. That one's a real doozy." Sam stared up at the sky and watched the sun peek out at them, his beautiful seafoam blue-green eyes deep in thought. "When your parents deem you old enough to join the sirens on your own, they basically kidnap you from your birthday party, take you anywhere in the world, and drop you off. You're expected to make your way home. If you don't make your way home, you're no longer part of the sirens. It's a fun family tradition," he added wryly.

Whitney couldn't help it. She reached out and took his hand. Talking about the sirens seemed fun and upbeat most of the time, but she was getting a good feeling there was a rift between Sam and his family. She didn't look at him as they laid there half in the water watching the clouds flutter by overhead.

"I was thirteen when my parents decided I was old enough. Most people don't do it until their children are fifteen or sixteen. That's why most of the sirens here are in high school and are typically juniors and seniors."

"Where did they leave you?"

"That's the kicker of it. Most parents want their children back, so they get left somewhere up the coast, maybe as far north as Maine or Canada, but not mine. Parents who really like their child just leave them on the other side of Florida in the Gulf. There is nice warm water, and easy access to home. My father actually asked for me to be left in the Pacific Ocean. He had me drugged and flown across the country, and as you know, most sirens don't want to go inland. It was real sweet he chose a place far away. I think he was secretly hoping I wouldn't make it back."

Whitney squeezed his hand. She couldn't imagine parents that wouldn't want their child back. She did her best not to think of her own parents that had been dead over a year now. She knew every day they were alive that they had wanted her, even if she didn't fit perfectly into the skinwalker night human world.

"But you did make your way back. You're here now."

Sam didn't answer as the water lapped at their elbows. The sea was slowly going back out. They wouldn't have much time left to talk for the day, and the next day was school. Whitney was more than a little disappointed.

"It took me weeks to make it home. I went inland a little bit to the first town I could find just to figure out where I was because I didn't recognize the fish in the area. I ended up off the coast of Oregon. I guess I should be glad he didn't put me in another country. He probably couldn't get someone to take that plane ride with the risk of getting stuck without water."

"Didn't they worry that you would be found? Aren't

sirens supposed to keep a secret?"

Whitney couldn't fathom being left on the other side of the US as a thirteen-year-old, let alone needing to make your own way home.

"That's kind of why I think he did it on purpose. If a hunter had found me, there was no way at that age I could fight back. Luckily I made it up a river into the town. It only took talking to one person, and she was my own age, so I wasn't worried that she was a hunter. I think she thought I was crazy or on drugs. I must have sounded crazy as I demanded to know where I was. When she went to find her mother, I took off again. Once I knew where I was, I made my way home."

Whitney tried to hide her surprise. She remembered that day. She was downtown with her mother shopping. Her mother had gone into an old lady store full of fluffy blouses and suits. Whitney didn't feel like tagging along and instead offered to wait at the bridge. Since her mother could see her from the store window and it was pretty much safe for any night human in town as they looked after each other, her mother agreed. Whitney sat on the bridge and threw stones in the river. She didn't notice the boy until he was standing beside her, wondering why she was throwing stones at fish. When she explained that it wasn't at fish, she realized he wasn't from town. He then demanded to know what town they were in. So yes, she remembered thinking he was crazy.

Watching the sky and trying not to give her thoughts away, Whitney kept her mouth shut about her memories. It would only bring more confusion into the whole thing if she added that anyway.

"Why wouldn't your dad want you home?" Whitney asked, avoiding the fact that she had been the girl. It was just too strange of a coincidence. She needed more time to think about that one. In the millions of places in the world he could have been left, and the multiple cities he could have swum to check, he had found her.

"I think it's because of my control. Even at a young age, I've been able to control my singing to not hurt people when controlling them. He's not that type of guy. He's a lot more like Tim. He thinks sirens should dominate with a hard hand. I don't do that, and he thinks I'm weak because of it. I proved to him that I'm not weak, but that didn't change anything." Sam rubbed the lines on his right arm.

"What are those tattoos?"

"My proof," Sam replied and pushed up into a sitting position. He didn't turn his fin into legs, yet had such an easier time of maneuvering than Whitney.

"There are several jobs you can choose from in the siren world. One of them is to join the guard. We protect the sirens from hunters." She had heard the term hunters several times now. She would have to ask for more details since she knew only the basics, but she didn't want him to stop talking as their time ran out. "When you join, if they accept you, you get one ring. When you pass the first test, you get a second ring. When you pass the last test, you get the third ring."

"Yet, you have four …" She had wondered more than once about those tattoos when he was teaching her how to swim.

"Because I passed a test no one else could pass in my batch of recruits. I'm the head of the guard currently … well, at least here on land. There's only one more test for me to pass to get the very head spot. I thought joining the guard would make my father see that I was as much a siren as Tim or any of my older brothers." Sam shrugged. "It didn't make a difference."

Sam pushed himself into the water. Whitney still had more questions, but the tide was going out. They had to leave.

"Do you feel hungry?" Sam asked.

How could she be hungry, they had eaten before they came in and had been there less than an hour. Sam waited as realization set in. He wasn't talking about food. Blushing from the thoughts of being pulled close to him again, she shook her head no.

"Then I'll feed tonight, and you can feed on me tomorrow. Can we meet by the pool after my lessons? I get done at 6:30. Will that work for you?"

His somber mood was completely gone now that they weren't talking about his family. He flashed a concerned smile, like he was trying to read her face to see if she was telling him the truth about being hungry. She really wasn't hungry and tried to convey that with the smile she gave in return.

Nodding, he dove further away. Sam was now fully in the water with just his head sticking out so he could talk. Whitney followed him even though she didn't want to. She wanted more time.

"Yeah, I have tomorrow night off from work." Whitney paused as the realization hit from her own words. She didn't have today off, and she was going to be late. Questions would have to wait. She dove under and made her way back out of the cove before Sam could reply.

CHAPTER 6

Sam drove as fast as he could to get Whitney to work on time. He didn't know she was supposed to be there. Otherwise he would have cut their question and answer time short. Whitney didn't have spending money since she began living with her aunt, so she needed the job. That much he knew and respected. Luckily, as they pulled into the parking lot of Bingos, they saw that Mark was working, too.

"Shoot," Whitney exclaimed as she dug through her bag, "I forgot to bring my shirt."

"You have a shirt on." Sam pointed out the obvious.

"No, we need to wear a white shirt," she explained.

Sam thought for a moment. He didn't want her to get in trouble on his account. And there was also the problem that he needed to be able to spend more alone time with her without anyone suspecting. He needed a really good excuse, especially if he wanted Mark to fall for it. Mark had known Sam all his life. They were the same age and had grown up together. Mark would be able to tell if he was lying, so it had to be really good.

"Let me talk to Mark. I'm sure he keeps backup shirts in the office. I've seen him not bring anything with him to work on many occasions," Sam replied, still racking his brain for a solution.

Whitney stepped out of the car, and Sam watched her as he moved to follow. She reached the door and pulled her hands through her hair, piling it up into a perfectly messy bun. That was Whitney. Even as she was faced with getting in trouble, she faced it head on. Or maybe she just trusted Sam. He liked that idea. Here she went off with him two days in a row and didn't ask where they were going or when they would get back. She had to trust him. He liked that about her, too. Who was he kidding? He liked everything about her and now that she was a siren, she was perfect. Now he just had to convince her that he was perfect for her too.

Sam grabbed the door to hold it open for hear. A plan fell into his head, and he was ready to be the one saving her. Yes, he was sure his plan was flawless.

"Hey, man," Mark said as he came up to them, looking at Whitney with questioning eyes.

"Would Whitney be able to borrow a shirt, so I don't have to drive her home and make her late? It's my fault," Sam began. Mark wiggled his eyebrows a little, and Sam was sure Whitney noticed.

"Sure. I have a few in the back."

Mark led the way to the break room. Sam had been there more than once. It was always where he had to sit and wait for Mark when they needed to be at concerts, and he didn't want to leave without making sure the place would run without him. Most sirens didn't care about anything on land, but it seemed like Mark cared more than a little for his job, even if he'd never admit it.

Opening a box by his desk, he pulled out a T-shirt and tossed it to Whitney. She took it with a grateful smile and headed into the only other door in the break room, the bathroom.

"Is she your new toy?" Mark asked quietly.

Sam grinned at Mark. He needed to make it seem like he didn't really care for Whitney and play along, even if it was far from the truth. If the sirens thought Whitney was just a fling, no one would care. Siren were allowed to date day humans on land food. If they thought he was serious about her, then they would look closer and for the reasons why. He didn't need people looking closer at her. She still didn't have full control of her siren, and that made things a bit hard for the time being.

"I think I have her convinced to *date* me," Sam told him. Mark wiggled his eyebrows.

"Man, you owe me big time. You get a girl that's hot and available anytime you want." Mark was only really a little jealous no matter how it sounded. He had tried several times to get Whitney to date him and she always turned him down. She was fair game for any siren until she said yes to one.

Whitney came back out; the shirt was a little big, but she had it tied in a knot, showing off a little bit of her tanned hip. Sam walked over and plopped his arm around Whitney. She stared up at him and didn't have her normally witty comeback since he had surprised her.

"I was just telling Mark that you were about to say yes to dating me like I asked earlier, and he completely approves," Sam told her, hoping she would get the drift of his statement and play along.

"Mmm." Whitney glanced at Mark and then slid her arm around Sam's waist. "I didn't know we needed his approval."

Mark laughed. "Whitney, you have the even number tables on the left side of the buffet tonight."

Whitney gave a mock salute before hurrying out the door and back into the restaurant.

"You so owe me," Mark commented as he passed Sam, following her out. "I've never had a blood bag that hot."

Finally alone, Sam let out his breath. He would have to explain it all to Whitney when they finally got the chance to be alone. It was the perfect cover. Sirens often took day human girlfriends when they didn't want to find more people to feed on—easy food. No one would blink an eye at it. He hoped. There was the fact that he had never had a day human girlfriend, but there was a first time for everything. At least it was the best plan he could come up with. He would have unlimited alone time with Whitney, and no one, well no siren, would find it odd. And there was the part where he would get to pretend she was his girlfriend, even if she wasn't. It was a win-win in his eyes.

Whitney didn't have time to sit around and listen to the guys talk more, but as she started her shift and took her first tables, she did hear Mark describe her as a blood bag. From what she could tell it wasn't strange that Sam was dating her, but she couldn't wait to get him alone and ask him what the heck that all meant. It wasn't like he asked her to date him. He just said it without her opinion, and she had to play along for now. Sam gave her an exaggerated wave good-bye as he left her at work. Did he actually want to date her? She hadn't got that feeling from him any time they had ever talked, so he must have just been a really good actor.

She spent the evening focusing on not dropping any plates of food on the floor, and by the time she got home she was exhausted enough to just fall in bed and sleep all night. Before she knew it, she was back in school again, and she found herself sitting in class wondering where her weekend went. Okay, she knew where it went because she had spent most of the time with Sam learning about being a siren or in her bathtub trying to get her legs back. That made for a quick weekend.

Making it through her Monday morning classes was torture. She really wanted to ask Sam what the heck was going on since she didn't have the time to call him the night before, and there were no messages in the morning. And there was the fact as she walked the halls at school that it seemed Mark was so nicely sharing with everyone that they were dating. She still had no idea why Sam had told his friend that.

"You know that even though you still owe him meals, it doesn't mean you have to date him," Tina said as Whitney joined her at lunch. Tina tossed her dark braid over her shoulder as she looked at Whitney, seeming genuinely concerned.

"That isn't it," Whitney replied.

"Ah huh," Trudy added as she sat on the other side of Whitney. "Haven't you seen how she looks at him? It was only time before he noticed also."

"Looks at him?" Whitney asked. She had been trying her best all year not to look at him.

She was more than happy Sam wasn't at lunch, so she didn't have to figure out if she was supposed to do or even what it meant to be dating him. As his pretend girlfriend, was she supposed to sit at his lunch table or hold his hand in the hallway? She really had no clue. She kind of got the feeling from everyone around her she either had to fake break up or go along with it. Not a single person questioned Sam dating her.

"You've been staring at him with puppy dog eyes for over a year now. Don't worry. I heard a rumor that Mark was assigned as your swim instructor, and Sam told him he wanted to teach you instead," Tina added, opening her bag lunch. "I think he's been crushing on you just as much as you on him."

Whitney kept her eyes glued to her lunch. She really didn't know what to say to that. Yeah, she thought Sam was cute, and maybe she had a little crush on him, but it wasn't what everyone thought. They weren't really dating. She was pretty sure that took two people to agree to and not just one making up their mind. And she was also pretty sure that Sam didn't like her. But what she didn't know was what his game was. Why was he telling people they were dating? She refused to let her heart beat a little faster at her friend's comment. Sam wasn't interested. Whitney was almost completely sure about that.

As lunch finished up, she realized she wasn't going to get an answer to her questions. Sam was a no-show, and all she saw when she looked over at the table was a very angry siren girl glaring at her. It seemed like there was one person who didn't like the news.

Whitney hurried off to class after lunch and was happy she had math. She couldn't daydream in math class if she wanted to pass. It wasn't that she found it hard, it was only if she didn't pay attention as the teacher taught that she struggled. It was a good distraction from her weird day.

The longest part of the day came when she had to spend three hours waiting to meet up with Sam. She was bursting with new questions and ready to give him a piece of her mind for deciding something like telling everyone they were dating without her. The eye wiggling and knowing looks Mark had given Sam the night before were mild compared to her day today. While it started out with whispers and people just talking, without Sam around all day, it turned into more than a few guys that would watch her as she passed. She had heard of feeling like a piece of meat, but she had the sense all the guys watching her were sirens. They were definitely thinking of her not as meat, but a source of blood. It got bad enough that by the time school ended, she was ready to find a place alone to sit and wait out the three hours.

Without heading home, Whitney made it to her favorite beach spot. It was quiet since the waves weren't rolling in enough to attract surfers, and the cloudy day meant that there were almost no beachgoers. In fact, if you asked her, it was perfect. She had the beach to herself.

Whitney sat in the sand, far enough away to not get sprayed by any water as she watched the slow waves rock back and forth onto land. It was sad to think she couldn't just wade ankle-deep through the water now with her new "condition", as she wanted to call it. Sam made it sound like all you had to do was think feet, but when she tried in the shower in the morning, she got nowhere. She still had a fin. She wasn't sure how long it might be, or even if she would ever be able to walk in water again.

The sun peeked out a bit through some clouds before hiding again, and she enjoyed the brief warmth on her skin.

It was strange to be a night human and enjoy the sun. Most of the night humans hid from it, but the mer didn't seem to be one of those kinds. There was much more she needed to learn. As she sat and watched the soft flowing froth from the waves, she began making a mental list of more questions. Would she ever have enough time to learn it all? Would Sam stick around long enough for her to ask everything she was thinking? Life would have been much easier if she was still home with her family. It would have been easier also if she had been born a siren. But she wasn't going to get either of those two options. Nope, her life had to be complicated.

Rising, Whitney dusted herself off. She would make it back before she was to meet him, but better early than late. At least she was trying for that to be her new motto. It hadn't caught on yet with her brain. She took one last look at the ocean before walking away. It was physically hard to leave it. She had loved sitting on the beach since she first arrived in Florida, but now it felt like an almost impossible pull that wanted her to stay right there and hop in the water. One more thing to talk to Sam about. She was piling more and more questions onto her plate as every moment passed. Hopefully, she would get more time to ask questions.

Using all her strength to walk away, Whitney began her twenty-minute walk back to school. She was able to get lost again in her thoughts as she walked the well-worn pathway off the beach and to the sidewalks. But it was harder to think thoughts as she walked away and the song of the ocean called to her. Luckily Whitney was a stubborn person, and she wasn't going to let the ocean win. She continued to walk and focus on her path to the school, not the place she was leaving.

Whitney walked around to the back of the school and the outdoor pool. The first gate was locked, and she expected that, but since she had been taking lessons the second gate hadn't been, and she continued over to it. Sure enough, Sam had the gate propped open with a shoe, like always.

She made her way around the bleachers; yes, her school pool had bleachers. She thought it was crazy at first, but then she found out that they had a competitive swim team, and the pool was gifted by an anonymous donor. She had a feeling, judging by who used it the most, the donor had to be a siren, but that was just one more questions to ask. Thankfully, it was almost time for answers.

Whitney walked down the hill and lost sight of the pool. Sam was still teaching his lesson, and she didn't want to interrupt him. As she rounded the path that led back up to the opposite side of the pool from the school, she heard soft singing coming from it. IT was soft, but she heard it. She kept off the path and hid behind the open gate, keeping herself from full view of the pool, but she saw through the cracks of the peeling paint that Sam was in the water. Mesmerized, she watched him dip his head to the water and into what was more than likely a student. She turned away as she finally found herself staring at what seemed like a very private moment, and she couldn't see beyond the top of his head.

Whitney remained in her hiding spot and didn't look to see which student was walking away. She didn't want to know who he was feeding on. She turned and waited for the student to leave and heard Sam say goodbye to them. When she heard the door to the school open and close, she meant to move out of her hiding spot but froze in her tracks.

The siren that had been staring daggers at Whitney all lunch, Amber, was walking up the pathway. Okay, it was more of a saunter than a walk. Considering she was wearing at least four-inch heels, Whitney was beyond shocked. No one walked around town in heels, at least not the teens. Whitney had changed out of her uniform when she left school, but like everyone else in their right mind when you know there's a beach around every corner, and more than likely where you'll end up, she was wearing sandals, a lot more practical. But then again, from the swaying of Amber's hips, as she walked past Whitney in her hiding spot, Whitney had a feeling the heels were intentional.

"Sammy," Amber cooed as she walked up to the pool.

Sam was already out of the water and drying off. He reached for his shirt to put back on, but Amber *accidentally* stepped on it and didn't seem like she would be moving. Amber leaned down in her low-cut top to pick up Sam's shirt for him. Sam watched her.

"I've heard a really strange rumor today," Amber continued.

Sam shrugged like it was nothing to him.

"That you went and asked a day human to be your girlfriend." Amber now visibly pouted.

Taking his shirt, Sam turned and put it back on. He turned back to Amber while sitting down to slip on his shoes and his back was to Whitney. She didn't hear his response, but from the expression on Amber's face, she wasn't happy.

"Mark said you are just having a bit of fun with her and wanted an easy feed, but you didn't have to stoop to that level. I could have had at least a dozen more people sign up for swim lessons if you needed the blood. All I'd have to do is ask them. No one likes to tell me no." Amber seemed to not like the news that had been spreading around the school, even if it was all made up. "If you need something else of a physical nature, I can take care of that."

Sam stood up as she talked, and Amber moved closer. She placed her arms up around his neck to hold him in place. Whitney felt a bit of anger beginning to boil in her. Yes, they were only pretend dating, but the siren didn't know that. In fact, Amber was hitting on Sam while knowing completely well that he was dating. Wasn't that just wrong? Who went around hitting on someone else's boyfriend? Then again, was there something going on with Amber and Sam? Whitney wished she saw Sam's face, but maybe not. What guy in their right mind wouldn't mind a beautiful girl like Amber throwing herself at him? What if they were really dating and keeping it a secret? Whitney's mind raced with questions that caused her anger to simmer into confusion.

"You smell delicious," Amber said as she leaned in near him.

Whitney clenched her fists as she watched. Amber was just too close to Sam. Logically Whitney had no right to Sam, and she shouldn't care what he did with whomever; it just felt like he was cheating on her. His hands rested on Amber's hips as he said something back to her. She smiled as she pulled back from his ear.

"Fine," she replied, giving him a little pout that wasn't a pout at all. "I'll play this game, but only for the week. You know your parents have been talking to my parents. I'm pretty sure they're arranging everything as we speak."

Sam said something else, and this time Amber gave a real pout.

"You're really not going?" she asked.

Again, Whitney was left in the dark. The siren world was confusing enough; she didn't have time to ask about the social and political aspects of what was going on. She had no clue what their parents talking meant. Just more questions to ask Sam, if she ever got time alone with him.

Sam talked some more and then finally Amber pulled back from him, keeping her hands to herself. Whitney felt a bit better, like the anger she felt at Amber was lessening … well, only a little. The extremely beautiful siren was still standing there keeping Whitney from getting time with Sam.

"Fine. I'll leave. But just know that once you're my mate, you won't have a mistress like that day human."

Amber leaned forward and kissed Sam before pulling back and grinning, like she had won the best prize in the world. Slowly she sauntered away, not turning around, but obviously walking with the intention of being watched.

Whitney stayed in her hiding place while Amber disappeared. Holding her breath, she counted to ten. It didn't help. Here she thought Sam cared enough to teach her how to be a siren. He never once mentioned that he had a future mate. Whitney had been around night humans her whole life. She knew what a mate was. It was a person you bonded yourself to for life. She knew exactly what it meant, and it meant no matter how cute he was or how much attention he gave her, it would end the minute he was mated to Amber. He wouldn't be able to hide things from her, and Whitney would be in danger. All the lessons would have to finish up in a week's time, and she would be on her own, again.

She let out her breath and tried counting once more, squeezing her eyes shut. She was stupid. Here she had just spent hours thinking about Sam and the world he brought her into. She thought about how her friends had teased her that he was always watching her. She had herself believing there was more between them than there really was. Yep, her life sucked. She went from being an outcast in the skinwalker night human world to now being one in the siren world. At least the skinwalkers never threatened to kill her for existing. Wasn't the point of moving away to start all over? She felt like she was back to where she was her whole life—part of the night human world, but outside it at the same time.

"Are you going to hide here all day?" Sam asked, and Whitney finally opened her eyes.

"Um, no," Whitney replied, trying to sound confused even though there was still a bit of anger and sadness all mixed inside of her. She walked around the fence and headed toward the pool bleachers to sit down.

Looking into his beautiful brown eyes, she could admit it now, but it made no difference. She had been falling for him, but he already had someone else. Someone much better suited for him. A real siren, someone who wouldn't be a problem, someone he wouldn't have to keep hidden. She had thought that because she had met him years ago as a kid that maybe it was fate telling something to her, but that was a lie, too. It was just a coincidence.

Sam grabbed her arm. Whitney froze when he touched

her. He had touched her a hundred times while teaching her how to swim, and then again as he pulled her through the underwater maze to the beach cove they had visited over the past few days, but something now felt different. She felt a zing as the sharp tingles zapped up her arm. Sam must have felt it also, because the expression on his face was that of complete surprise.

"More special powers?" Whitney asked as she took her arm back and rubbed the spot.

"Something like that." Grinning at her, Sam held out his hand for Whitney to take. She raised an eyebrow at him. What game was he playing now?

"What, my girlfriend won't hold my hand?" he gave a fake pout.

"About that," Whitney said.

Sam's eyes got wide. He quickly leaned close to whisper in her ear.

"Play along with me, please. I'll explain everything in five minutes once I get us alone and away from prying eyes and ears."

Whitney's eyes shot open wide, and she lifted her head to look around. They were being watched? Good thing she hadn't said anything that would give away she knew about the siren, and better that she hadn't jumped in the pool and gone all fishy.

Sam didn't offer her his hand again. Instead, he pulled her close to him so that their bodies were only millimeters apart, his arms wrapped around her back to keep her from moving away. He kissed her neck and sent shivers to her toes.

"Please help me convince them we're actually dating," Sam said quietly enough that Whitney barely heard. "Just pretend you're wildly in love with me."

Whitney's heart beat hard. It wouldn't take much pretending. Now, with his arms wrapped around her, it almost felt like she could feel the love from him. It was crazy as her logical mind told her that it was all a game, and that he already had a siren girlfriend, or rather, soon-to-be mate, but her heart and hands said screw it. She wrapped her arms around him, too.

Sam kissed up her neck again, hiding his words with kisses to anyone that was watching. Pulling back, he gazed down at her. His eyes begged her to play along, and Whitney could almost say there was more in his eyes than just a plea. It had to be wishful thinking.

She reached her hands up to run them through his still-wet hair, which looked almost jet-black as the sun sparkled off it. Smiling, Sam leaned into her touch like a cat would and that made her smile more.

"Fine," she said quietly, giving into his pleading.

Sam grinned and didn't give her a chance to change her mind as he dipped down and pressed his lips to hers. It surprised Whitney, but that didn't mean she wasn't about to kiss him back. In fact, her lips made up their own mind, and before she knew it, she was wrapped in his arms, sharing an incredible kiss. She had kissed guys before—that was nothing new—but this kiss with Sam was perfect. Their lips felt like they were made for each other.

He pulled back just inches, keeping his nose to hers as he smiled at her. Whitney hadn't wanted the kiss to end and kept her arms wrapped around him. She tugged gently at his head, and he got the message as he moved back down to kiss her again. Yes, the second kiss was just as great as the first. And somehow it turned into a third and a fourth, and she lost track of time.

Caught in the bliss that was Sam's lips, Whitney found herself being carried away from the pool, their lips never breaking as Sam moved down the hill toward the school. Sam finally broke the kiss by setting her down outside the door to the boys' locker room as he dug out keys from his pocket. Whitney leaned against the brick wall and caught her breath while she watched him.

She wanted to look around and see if their audience left, but then she would be all done with the incredible make-out sessions with Sam and have to go back to the real world where they weren't actually dating.

With the door open, Sam threw his bag and Whitney's into the locker room. She didn't remember him picking them up at the pool, but now her eyes went big.

"Hey, that's the boys' locker room," she complained. She was going to have to go in to get her bag, and she hoped because it was locked no one would be around.

Sam's teeth sparkled as he smiled at her. "Yep, and I happen to have a key to use it after hours." He swung his key chain around on his finger.

Whitney gave him her best "and so" face, hoping he would explain more before she broke their façade of a happy, in-love couple.

"And we can be completely alone since I'm the only one that uses it after hours until swim season starts next fall."

Ahh, Whitney got it. They could be alone, and that was just what they needed for her to continue learning about the sirens. She grinned up at him. He had thought it all out perfectly. Even if he was a bit bossy, at least he was smart. It didn't mean she was going to just do as he said now that she understood that better, but it was nice to know.

Sam stepped back over to Whitney, trapping her against the wall with his arms on either side of her face. She looked up at him and felt her heart thump in her chest at him being close. It was going to be a long afternoon learning about sirens if she kept wanting to kiss him and relive their little act from before. Shoot, who was she kidding? Whitney hadn't been acting, even if Sam had. Oh well, she would enjoy it while it lasted and hoped that maybe his siren shadows would follow him around some more so they could get another perfect kiss in.

She didn't have to wait for a moment as Sam's head swooped down and his lips found their way back to her. Sam pressed her to the wall and pulled her legs up to wrap around him. Without a look back, he marched them into the locker room and locked the door behind them. Whitney sighed, thinking the kiss would be done, but he didn't stop. He passed their bags on the floor and around the corner to the showers. Sitting down, he expertly moved her legs around so that she was sitting across his lap now. He broke the kiss only to reach back and turn the water on in the shower behind them. The light mist that made its way to them instantly turned Whitney's legs to a fin. Sam turned them around so that her tail could feel the water as it ran over it. He ran his hand down her pink fin, causing a new burst of tingles throughout it and right down to the edge where her toes used to be.

Sam pulled Whitney to his chest and tucked her under his chin. He gave a sigh himself before finally letting go of her and setting her down on the bench beside him.

Whitney noticed his guilty expression.

"Your girlfriend isn't going to be mad at you?" she asked. Whitney wanted to smack her head. She really knew how to put her foot in her mouth, but she just couldn't help it.

Something inside her made her upset to be the cause of his sadness. She had no idea where that feeling was coming from, but it was strong. Sam was sad, and she felt it as she sat beside him. It was almost tangible.

"Girlfriend? You're my girlfriend. Are you mad at me?" he asked with a slight grin.

Whitney slapped his chest playfully, hoping he would get back to being the normal, happy Sam and not the sad one that had magically appeared after a great kissing session that was done way too early, if you asked Whitney.

"Your siren girlfriend," she replied while rolling her eyes. At least that had cheered him up as he smiled at her, but now he seemed a bit confused. "You know, your future mate?"

Whitney didn't understand where the confusion was

coming from. He had just been talking to her.

"Amber," she added since it didn't seem like he understood.

Sam broke out laughing, not the reaction Whitney was expecting. Nothing she said was funny.

"Amber as my girlfriend?" He laughed some more, enough to shake the bench they were both sitting on. "She's been trying for years, but I've always told her no. We grew up together. I will never see her as anything more than a sister. She might want more, and possibly pushed her parents for it, but it will never happen. Amber is just Amber," Sam told her, like it explained everything. He pretty much explained nothing that made any sense.

"It didn't look like that before," Whitney added under her breath, and Sam grinned more at her.

"You're jealous," he teased.

Whitney's face turned red and thankfully the water pouring onto her tail was hot, so she was going to blame her face on that.

"Of what? I'm only your pretend girlfriend." Whitney tried to keep the pout out of her voice as she willed her face to remain neutral.

"Only if you want it to be pretend," Sam replied, as he touched her red cheek gently.

CHAPTER 7

Sam stared into Whitney's eyes and tried to read what was going on behind them. Normally she was an open book, even when she tried to hide her feelings. Sam had spent over a year watching her. He knew when she was sad. He knew when she was mad. He knew when she was happy. No one else might have noticed, but after studying her enough, he did. But now her eyes were guarded. She was purposely hiding her feelings from him.

"Are you saying that because you really like me, or are you saying that to piss everyone off?"

Sam couldn't help the corners of his mouth from starting to move on their own. Just one more reason he liked her: she was smarter than anyone ever gave her credit for. She had noticed the effect of their relationship. Most girls would not have picked up on it, but she did.

"I'm not trying to upset the sirens. That's me refusing to go home for my birthday. That's trying to upset them. You …" Sam trailed off.

He just didn't know how to put it without coming off as creepy. He had been watching her over a year and wanting to have her as his the whole time. Then again, she probably already found him creepy. He had been feeding on her for over a year under the guise of teaching her how to swim, which he actually did very well, and he had been the person to change her back into a monster. She probably didn't want to actually be his girlfriend.

Looking back into her eyes, he made the choice. He was brave when facing hunters. He was brave when facing his father, King of the Sirens. He was brave when facing his older brothers who had beat on him unmercifully when he was growing up. He was going to be brave while facing Whitney, the hardest thing he had ever had to do.

"Whitney," Sam said slowly as he thought of the words to say.

She was staring down at her fin as it flapped in the water. Again, he found himself smiling. She was a siren now, and no one could stop them if she actually wanted to be with him, too. And based on the kisses she had given him just moments before, he had to hope that meant she wanted him, too. He reached over and touched her chin gently, turning her face up so that their eyes locked.

"I've spent my whole life in the mer world, looking and searching for a mate. It's tradition that if you don't choose by your eighteenth birthday, your parents will choose a mate for you. You get no say, and you get someone you are stuck with for the rest of your life. I knew from the time I was dropped off in the Pacific I wasn't going to let my parents choose. They haven't ever had my best interest at heart. I needed to find my own mate. So I searched. I've looked and looked. I've been on hundreds of dates to know that each girl I ever met wasn't for me. I went outside of the sirens knowing my parents would be upset, but they would eventually get over it as long as she had a fin. My life has been a series of work and dates, and yet I never found a girl that I felt even an ounce of what I feel for you."

Whitney's eyes went wide as he admitted his feelings. She didn't reply or run away shrieking, and he took that as a sign to continue. Okay, she couldn't exactly run away with her fin sitting there in the water, but she wasn't shrieking.

"When you came to school here, it was like I felt as if I had met you before. I was drawn to you like I never had been to a girl before. Something about you was familiar, and I wondered why. I began to watch you."

Quickly, Sam put a finger on her lips to keep her quiet. He didn't know if he would have the nerve to say more if she interrupted him, and he needed to get it all out there. She needed to know this wasn't just a ploy to upset the sirens; she needed to know what he felt was real.

"The more I watched you, the more I wanted to know you better. When you asked to do swimming lessons and the school assigned you to Mark, I made him switch. I'm kind of in charge here, so I just had to say I wanted to teach you, and he had to obey. He thought it was because of how beautiful you are, but in reality, I saw much more of you beyond your looks."

Whitney bit her lip as he talked—a nervous reaction of hers. Sam rubbed his finger on her cheek, hoping to send calming vibes her way.

"You are beautiful, but you are also smart, caring, funny, and clever all rolled into one. The mer don't look at day humans as anything but food and I should have done the same, but I couldn't with you. More than anything, I wanted to get to know you better. I wanted to spend time with you. I wanted you to finally look at me and see me for me as you did your friends. You are the first day human they have ever befriended. And I knew that was because it was you. Something about you makes the mer see more in day humans. You are special."

Whitney tried to avert her gaze, but Sam kept firm and held her face up looking at him. She didn't like being complimented on anything but her appearance. He needed to finish up because it was torture to not know what she thought.

"I'm not here asking you to be my mate. That's a commitment I can't ask of you." *At least not at this time*, he thought to himself. "What I'm asking is that if you feel anything for me, to give me a chance to prove to you I should be your boyfriend. I'm sorry that I'm the one who turned you, and if you just want to stay as friends because deep down you can never forgive me, I'll understand."

Sam let go of her face and turned to the spray of water. He hadn't meant to add the last part about turning her, but he needed to give her an out in case she didn't have feelings for him like he thought she did. He might have imagined the whole thing with wishful thinking.

Stretching and wiggling his toes, he let his fin appear next to hers. Her fin wiggled a bit beside his. Old legends had said that when you found your destined mate, you would know. That's why the sirens put such an emphasis on finding your mate before you turned eighteen. Sam sucked in a breath as her fin brushed against his. Even if she didn't want to date him, he couldn't stop wanting her. That was impossible. He had found his one and only.

"I like you, too," Whitney whispered, the words barely audible over the sound of the water hitting the shower around them.

Sam thought he must have been hearing things as his head snapped up, but then he felt it inside him like he had when they touched back at the pool. She had said it. She really had. Sam didn't think further and let his siren take over as he pulled her back onto his lap, back where she fit perfectly in his arms. Back where he hoped she would never leave.

Whitney walked around school the next day in a daze. The night before still seemed completely unreal. She had pinched herself more than a dozen times on her walk home, and even made Sam pinch her once for good measure. It wasn't a dream. Sam really liked her. She now had her first ever boyfriend. Her fake boyfriend was her real boyfriend. That wasn't easy to believe.

They hadn't had much time to talk since most of the time they'd spent with their lips already busy, but he did have a chance to explain that the sirens would see her only as a snack and play toy. He was sorry that it would be that way, but they would leave him alone, and he could now spend as much time as he wanted with her without anyone catching on to the truth. His plan got them alone time whenever they wanted. She had to admit she was sad he hadn't thought of it earlier.

Now that everything was out in the open, she saw Sam a lot more at school than she realized. They didn't have any classes together, but it seemed like they had a lot of classes right next door to each other. She found that out as Sam walked her to each class and then was waiting outside the door when she left. When he said he'd been watching her since she came to the school last year, she now saw how he did it without her or anyone else knowing.

They didn't say much as they walked the hallways; Sam, being the gentleman he was, carried her books. She could feel the eyes of everyone on them as they went between classes. She couldn't remember a time that Prince Sam had a girlfriend. She had wanted to ask her friends as far back as last year, because they obviously knew the school and all the people in it better than she ever imagined, but she didn't want them to know she had a crush on him. In hindsight she didn't hide it that well as they already knew before she told them.

Her friends took the news and Sam hanging around in stride. It turned out that while they made comments about him behind his back, they didn't actually dislike him as much as they pretended. Without his normal group of friends around him as he walked her to classes—sometimes with Tina or Trudy—Sam actually fit in well with her friends. They also seemed to notice the difference and lightened up after their first day of warnings.

"Do you work tonight?" Sam asked when Whitney stopped at her locker before their last class of the day.

"No. Mark has off, and it seems like I've only been scheduled when he works," she replied.

She hadn't noticed when she started, but now that she knew who Mark really was, she kept better track of when he would be there since she had to be extra careful around him.

Going through her schedule, it really did look like he only scheduled her when he was there. Whether that was on purpose or not, she wasn't sure. Since she had started dating Sam, he had stopped asking her out. At least there was one siren who respected that they were dating. Amber was a whole other story. She glared at Whitney every chance she got.

"Good. Want to come with tonight?"

"I thought we were grabbing dinner and a walk on the beach," she replied. At least that was what she remembered him mentioning somewhere between kisses forty-two and sixty-four.

"I was hoping we could get a walk in before we have to catch the bus," Sam replied. "Someone canceled, and we got booked in their place. Short notice, but we tend to not turn them down if they're in the area."

Now she knew exactly what tonight meant. He had another gig. Whitney smiled. Hearing him sing the first time had been amazing, but hiding in the bus was a pain. She wasn't sure she wanted another trip sitting under the bench seat.

"Come with me as my guest," he clarified, as he also probably remembered their trip only days ago.

Smiling, Whitney nodded. She had been smiling all day and figured eventually her cheeks were going to hurt too much if she didn't stop soon. Sam smiled back at her and quickly kissed her cheek like he knew exactly what she was thinking.

"Have fun at class," he said as they had already reached the door.

She nodded in a daze and went into the room to find her seat. Unfortunately for her, her last class of the day was shared with Amber. She knew from the brief conversation with Sam that he didn't like Amber at all, but she could also tell that Amber really liked him. Whitney would have felt bad for her if she hadn't seen Amber throw herself at Sam the day before. Now she was more than a little fed up with her.

Whitney ignored the scowl on Amber's face as she passed her on the way to her seat. It was going to be a long class, emphasized by scowls from Amber every five minutes when she had some sort of excuse to look around the room. Whitney squared her shoulders and did her best to ignore the unhappy siren and pay attention to class, which was considerably harder than normal to do as her mind drifted to Sam again. At least thoughts of Sam made the class go faster, and it was done before she knew it. Then again, she was pretty sure she missed everything the teacher had said. It was going to mean more reading to catch up on, but so totally worth it.

Packing up her bag slowly, Whitney made sure she would be able to leave the school right away without having to go through her locker while Sam waited. It was a good day with very little homework, and she had gotten almost everything done in class. Even with the book chapter, she needed to read she'd be able to fake in English the next day, because she had read the book before. Certain she was ready to go, Whitney made her way back out of the classroom, expecting to see Sam waiting.

Well, he was waiting, but not as she expected. Amber was leaning toward him and trying to wrap her arms around him. Sam was expertly untangling himself as he spotted Whitney. Amber must have known that Whitney would be there as she tried a second time to get Sam cornered. Sam ducked and got away, leaving her in mid-sentence.

"Ready to go?" he asked, not so much as glancing back at the extremely ticked-off Amber.

"Yes," Whitney replied, half tempted to turn and give Amber a little wave as they walked away, but then thought better of it. She didn't need to be on her radar for anything other than just being with Sam. They both agreed the less the sirens wanted to know about her, the better off they would be.

"Let's hit the beach while the guys pack the bus," Sam suggested, leading her to his car.

Whitney raised an eyebrow at his ditching of his friends to do all the work.

"They already know I'm bringing you with," Sam explained as he opened the car door for Whitney. She hopped in, and he went around to his side.

"And they're fine doing all the lifting?" Whitney didn't need his bandmates angry with her, either. She already had one siren she was sure hated her guts.

"As long as we get back in an hour, they're fine. They think I'm feeding on you and luring you to the beach to do just that," Sam explained as he drove away from the school.

Whitney giggled. It was kind of amusing how wrong everyone was about it. Her life depended on them all thinking about it that way, but it was still funny. It was like living a double life. At least in each version, she got to be with Sam. He grinned like he knew why she was laughing as he drove down the street and to the beach they had gone to before.

"No wonder they know you by name," Whitney said as he parked at the diner and led the way down to the beach. "I'm surprised they haven't named a sandwich after you already."

"Ha, ha, ha," Sam said, pulling her behind him on the small pathway.

Taking her hand, Sam led the way to the beach. They weren't ten feet in when Sam paused and then pulled Whitney to the right side of the path. She didn't ask what was going on and trusted him. Just around the tree line where the tall grass started, a blonde head popped up as someone walked toward them. They stood to the side to let the leaving person pass. Sam didn't look at the man, but Whitney did. His blond hair was cut short, almost in a military buzz, but that wasn't what made him stand out. His blue eyes stared directly at them as he walked by. Sam gave him a friendly nod of the head, but the guy didn't even look at him. He continued to stare at Whitney. Whitney looked to Sam's back as he tugged her forward and that was a good thing. Suddenly, she was very cold. Blondie's stare had given her the shivers.

Sam didn't talk any more as they neared the waterline. Whitney walked toward the enticing waves, but Sam turned and took her down the beach instead. She looked at him, but he didn't talk; instead, they just walked hand in hand in the warm sand. When they made it around the bend, Sam finally slowed down and found a place to sit.

"No swimming today?" Whitney asked, finding the change in his character weird.

"I was planning on taking you into the cove to answer more questions, but sometimes you have to change your plans." His non-descriptive speech made her wonder if more people were around. Maybe some siren had followed them. She didn't see anyone on the beach, but she had the feeling she wasn't going to get more question and answer time, at least not right now.

"Did I do something?" Whitney really had no clue why the sudden change in his attitude.

Sam seemed to shake out of his thoughts and turned to smile at her.

"No. You've been perfect. It's nothing to worry about. I'll tell you all about it later. Now let's just enjoy sitting here in the warm sun," he suggested, pulling her to his lap and letting her lean back into his arms.

"Can I at least hear more about your family or this birthday you're avoiding? Maybe you can tell me more about where you're from. I haven't been allowed to travel since I've been living with my aunt," Whitney said, trying to keep things very non-specific.

Sam chuckled, making her bounce with his laugh. He pulled her close and kissed her cheek before threading his fingers through hers.

"Well, where I'm from is kind of small compared to the cities around here," Sam began. Whitney settled back to listen to him talk. "I think my city is maybe a couple thousand people at most. It's the kind of place where everyone knows everyone."

"And where parents expect you to hook up with their best friends' kids," Whitney supplied for him. Amber had been on her mind a bit since she was still throwing herself at him.

Sam laughed a second time and Whitney decided she really liked hearing him laugh. She was hoping they would get more time together so she could hear more of it.

"I'm going to guess you're talking about Amber. She doesn't compare to you, and she knows it. Don't let her get to you. I'm not going to allow them to decide my fate. I'm going to decide what I want, and my father will just have to learn to live with that."

"Sure," Whitney added. While it all sounded great— making your own choices—she had been a night human. They weren't always up for choices. But she did admire his determination.

Sam wrapped his free arm around Whitney's middle and pulled her closer.

"You can't imagine how long I've been looking for someone like you. Even if you've never met my family, you get it. You get the whole world I'm from without being there or being corrupted by them. My family …" Sam trailed off, and Whitney listened to the waves crash as he thought. "My family aren't good people. I mean, don't get me wrong, I love them. But they just aren't good people. Where I'm from there aren't a whole lot of nice people. I'm guessing it's because they think they're better than everyone around them, but for whatever reason, they treat everyone they think is too different as being lower than them. It's not how I wanted to live, and I was happy to move away."

"Is that why you don't want to go home for your

birthday?" Whitney asked. She had heard it mentioned more than once that he was boycotting.

She could feel him shrug without looking behind.

"I decided weeks ago I wasn't going back because that's when your parents decide who you'll marry if you didn't already choose someone. There's no one back there I want to marry, so what's the point? I know my father will be mad, but at the same time I have a job to do, and I can't do that from home. I figured he can get mad about me not coming home, but he can't get mad about me staying around to do my job."

"And what exactly is your job, besides teaching swim lessons and singing songs for fans that are throwing themselves at you?" Whitney asked. She didn't blame the fans one bit. She had thought he was gorgeous the first time she met him.

Sam didn't answer, but turned her around in his arms and met her with a kiss before she could ask more. He pulled back and grinned.

"I'd think you might be a little jealous of those fans," he teased.

"Jealous?" Whitney replied, raising an eyebrow. "I think you have that in reverse. Those fans should be jealous of me." She reached her hands up and pulled his face back for a kiss.

Sam leaned back in the sand, pulling her with him without breaking the kiss. Whitney was never one for large displays of public affection, but that didn't matter with Sam. There was just something about him. Every moment she saw him, she wanted to throw her arms around him and make sure everyone knew he was hers. And then as soon as she touched him, the whole world around them disappeared anyway.

His phone beeped in his pocket, bringing them back to reality. Sam sighed and pulled back from their kiss.

"Time to be responsible and go do my job," he

complained as he stood up, brushing sand off him before helping Whitney back up, too.

Whitney grinned as he took her hand. There were worse jobs to have than a rock star. Only someone like Sam would see it as only a job and not a fun time.

The bus ride, this time, was shorter, and Whitney was glad. The guys all seemed really curious about her and asked a whole lot of questions. She did her best to answer, but some had to be deflected. Mostly they were looking for how she won Sam over. They let it slip more than a few times that Sam was too devoted to his family to think of dating. They really were curious as to how she changed his mind. And it was mostly Mark. Leo asked a few questions here and there, but Mark was the one that wouldn't let up. It took a hard glare and a bit of an order from Sam to get him to let it go.

After the question and answer session, Whitney spent the remainder of the time pulled to Sam's side while he and the guys discussed the set for the show. She had almost no clue what they were talking about and found it fun to simply watch them.

When she looked at Sam's two friends, she didn't see the siren in them. They looked and acted much like day humans; she couldn't fault herself for not seeing it before. Mark was your typical surfer guy with a laid-back personality that seemed to agree with everything being said to him when he wasn't asking a question. Leo was much quieter. He thought more about things, but again would never question Sam. Both guys seemed more than willing to follow Sam's lead, and that was the only night human trait she saw in them. Where she was raised, there was always an alpha that people followed. Sam kind of filled a role like that now that she listened in and saw it.

As they finished their plans, Sam pulled her tight into his

arms, and she got to spend the last half hour snuggled up to him. It was definitely a better ride than the last time.

Once they reached the place they were playing, the guys were all busy. Whitney was given a backstage pass, and she watched from the sidelines as the guys set up and did voice check. She was content to sit and watch, and once they were done, Sam pulled her back to the bus to be alone with her as the audience arrived. This time, the guys left them alone.

"Are you sure they won't come back here?" Whitney asked for the tenth time as Sam was hopping in the hot tub in their bus.

A hot tub in the bus seemed weird only days ago, but now completely normal. The band was part fish, so, of course, they needed a hot tub on their bus.

"I promise. I ordered them to stay out, and they have to listen to me." Sam offered his hand to Whitney. She looked at the front of the bus one last time and then decided that she trusted Sam wouldn't let her get caught.

Sam held her waist as she threw both her feet over the edge at the same time, knowing they would be an instant fin. She didn't want to see if it was painful to turn one foot at a time. Knowing her luck, it wouldn't be painful but snap her second leg into place, and she would crash into the water as ungraceful as she could be at times. Sam didn't need to see that side of her yet.

"Have you tried to will them to stay legs?" Sam asked.

How did he know she had been practicing each morning in the shower?

"Still not working?" Sam guessed.

Whitney hung her head and shook it no. She had been trying, and it stunk. She was normally a natural at things. Even the mer stuff was easy. After her first swim with Sam, she didn't even question breathing underwater. Or swimming underwater. Or swimming with a fin. Those things just felt right. But managing her tail wasn't one of those naturally easy things.

Sam tipped her face back up with just one finger on her chin. Whitney did her best to hold in her sigh. His touch was more enticing when she was in her siren form. Something about either being a half-fish, or maybe it was being wet in the water that made it all feel different. Sam must have noticed as his eyes flashed to their sea color as he transformed also. Whitney's sigh caught in her throat. He was a beautiful human, but he was a stunning merperson. The deep brown lines on his arm almost shimmered, but the intricate tattoos that ran from his shoulders down to his fin were fascinating. Whitney tried to keep her face from blushing as she looked at them and then realized where she would be looking if he were still in his swim trunks. Sam grabbed hold of her and pulled her to his lap, his blue fin rubbing against her pink one, sending a whole new sensation to the tip of her tail.

"I wish I could sit in here with you all day," Sam told her, his hand tracing the lines on her skin and stopping as he traced all the lines on her shoulder.

Whitney had looked at the lines that appeared on her as a mer and was more than happy to see it covered all the basic upper body parts to not leave her naked and he only stopped because of where he would be touching and not that they had disappeared. The shimmery purple color of the lines complemented her pink fin nicely as they swirled around her body. Now she knew what her back must have looked like also as Sam's fingers trailed over her shoulder. She had yet to be able to get a mirror behind her to see what it looked like.

"You amaze me every time I see you transform," Sam said quietly, his voice barely audible over the noises around them.

"Haven't you seen like a million girls turn into fishies?" Whitney teased.

Sam chuckled. He at least found her term "fishies" funny, but the other mer would take offense. With their view on order and being at the top, the siren didn't like being compared to mere fish, not quite the bottom of the ladder, but pretty close. Sam didn't take offense to anything. He was helpful and tried his best with everything she was going through.

"No, I have not. I don't know a million girls. But yes, I've seen others transform." Sam thought for a moment. "I don't know what's different, but you are different. I mean the pink fin is one thing, but beyond that. There's something else that just seems amazing."

Whitney glanced at her salmon-colored fin and wondered what it meant. He had explained a bit about the blues and greens in the siren world, but he never told her about the other types of mer. Was he leaving something out? He did say he would marry any type of mer.

"Could it be I'm not a siren?" Whitney asked. She had been wondering that since she got her siren anatomy lesson, or rather, levels of power lesson.

"No. I'm certain you're a siren. Besides, you already told me that you put your cousin into a trance while singing. That should prove it to you."

Okay, that much was true. She was pretty sure she was a siren also, and she had kept her mouth locked shut when she got the urge to sing with any song on the radio. Now that she might snap and eat someone, she refused to sing outright. She wasn't about to tell Sam she was listening to his orders, even though she was.

"There's just something magical about how you transform. It's almost like you sparkle as you do it, and you should see your eyes. They turn the most beautiful shade of purple I've ever seen."

He was now staring intently at her. Whitney tried not to smile, but she couldn't help it. The awe she saw in his eyes was exactly the same as she felt when she looked at him. She wanted to pretend it was a siren thing, but she was pretty certain it was a Sam thing. The more they were together, the more she realized she was falling hard for him. It wasn't just the awesome kisses. It was beyond that. There was something that made her not want to let him go anywhere without her.

Sam broke eye contact and tilted his head to the side. He shook his head disappointedly.

"I have to head back with the guys. We have to go over the set again and everything," Sam told her as he turned and lifted her out of the hot tub, leaving her tail in the water.

Whitney flicked her tail over the edge and let it drip as Sam jumped out of the tub with legs. She really needed to learn that trick. Sam waved his hand, and all the water went back in the tub, including the last drop falling from her tail. That was another trick she needed to learn. Sam reached for a towel and handed it to her. Whitney blotted off the few damp spots left on her tail, and her legs reappeared.

"You can hang out on the bus if you want or backstage. The pass will basically work anywhere to get in," Sam explained, slipping a shirt on.

"Can I go into the audience?"

"You might want to stay closer to the stage. The people toward the back are always drinking and spilling their drinks when they have too much. And since the stage is covered, even if it starts to rain you should be safe in the front of the arena. The back isn't covered."

"Played here before?" Whitney guessed. Sam grinned as he nodded, offering her a hand to go with him.

Whitney took his hand and let him pull her out of the bus. She looked up to the darkening sky and knew it was a combination of night time and possible storms. At least the bus was under some sort of awning that they could go from the stage to the bus without getting wet if it rained. She really needed to learn how to control her fin. That was priority number one.

Mark was waiting just inside the doors as they passed two very large security men. They didn't look at the pass around

Whitney's neck, but then again, she was walking in with the lead singer of the band that was going to go on soon. It was chaos as people ran from place to place backstage, but Sam didn't seem to notice. He took the guitar from Mark and slung it around his neck.

"Stay safe," Sam whispered in her ear as he leaned down to kiss her and give her hand one last squeeze before he turned to Mark. Whitney nodded, giving him the reassurance that she would be as he walked away.

Whitney didn't follow Sam and Mark as it was kind of fun just to watch everything around them. She passed through an open door and around a corner to follow the noise she heard from people. Signs pointed to the backstage and security dotted the hallways, so she wasn't worried about getting lost. Sam had mentioned on the ride that there was a VIP section near the front of the stage that her pass would get her into, and his warning of the rain coming was enough to keep her from going out to the main audience.

Following the signs, it wouldn't be difficult to find the VIP section, and she made her way up the stairs. She realized that the maze she was walking around had been underground which explained why the noise was muted. As she opened the door above ground, she heard the voices increase ten-fold. A large, beefy man stood behind the door she had just opened. He looked down at her pass and nodded to her, pointing to a door on the right. Following his direction, she made her way to the VIP lounge.

Opening the red door led to an unexpected lavishly decorated room. There were red velvet couches that a few people lounged on and a table set up on the far wall filled with a variety of foods that looked almost as artistic as edible. Whitney wasn't hungry. Actually, since she had turned into a siren she had found her need for actual food decreased a lot. She looked over the room and didn't glance at the people. It wasn't like she was going to know anyone. Passing the couches, she continued toward the noise. A hallway on the right side of the room was actually a connection to seats right at the edge of the stage. Whitney smiled. She was going to get the best seats in the house to watch her boyfriend sing. Yep, her life was beyond surreal now.

Whitney sat down and pulled out her phone. There were no messages from her aunt. She probably didn't check if she was home. At least her cousin knew she was out, so she wouldn't get in trouble in the small chance that Aunt Marissa came looking for her. It was only a very small chance. There were messages from both Trudy and Tina. They obviously didn't approve of Sam taking her out of town, but wanted to know where they were going on a date. When she had texted them earlier about it being a concert, they both agreed that was a cool date to go on and were a bit jealous. She left off the part of Sam singing, as she didn't know if she was supposed to tell them. She'd have to ask Sam after the show if they or any of the other sirens knew.

The lights dimmed around her to tell everyone that the guys were going to take the stage soon. The audience's excitement was almost palpable. Whitney tucked her phone away and grinned along with all the energy that was building. She had caught a little of the guys singing before, and she had heard of the group without knowing it was them, but to be there sitting and seeing it live was much more exciting.

The stage cut to black and from her seat she could see the guys enter, even if those further away couldn't. She didn't need to be told which one was Sam because she just felt it. The audience screamed as the drums began their beat with Mark's bass strumming along with it. The energy around them grew as the beat grew louder. Whitney wondered how she would hear over the crowd, but it was like someone was slowly turning up the volume. She felt the music reverberate inside her all the way down to her bones, but the part that took her breath away was when the lights turned to the stage.

Sam was standing there in ripped jeans and a tight black shirt, showing off every perfect chest muscle he had. He looked absolutely flawless, and Whitney wasn't the only one who thought that. Practically every female in the audience gave a collective sigh.

Sam leaned forward to the mic and began to sing. Whitney leaned forward at the same time and closed her eyes. His voice was perfect. She let it flow over her and listened to the words of the song. It took until the second song in to realize all his songs were about love. Really? He was a rock star singing about love. How more cliché could he get? Whitney opened her eyes as the song changed, and Sam had stepped back to play a solo on his guitar. A guitar playing, perfectly chiseled, rock star merman boyfriend. Whitney's life was never going to be the same. Any kind of life after Sam was going to be dull.

Whitney's heart ached a bit. She already knew it was true. There was going to be life without Sam at some point. He was a siren, and he had explained that they all went back to the island eventually. She wasn't part of it. She was an outsider, and someday he would have to go back. She shook her head to try to get rid of all the sad thoughts. Sam seemed to sense her and pointed at her to get her attention as he sang. He winked and that brought a smile to her face. She was going to just live in the moment and enjoy it.

The guys finished their set, and Whitney stood to go back downstage to meet them. The rain had luckily stayed away, and she was happy to not have to worry about that. The crew came on and began changing out the gear for the next group.

"Leaving so fast?" someone said from beside her. Whitney hadn't noticed all the VIP seats by the stage were filled.

Turning to the person speaking, she stopped in her tracks.

Sam's older brother, Tim, was sitting there beside her, maybe he had even been the whole time. He looked eerily similar to Sam; it would be hard to not guess they were related, but what got Whitney was when she looked in his eyes. Sam's always took her breath away. His eyes were kind and gentle. There was nothing like that behind Tim's eyes. Tim smiled in a welcoming manner, but his eyes were anything but friendly.

"I need to get backstage so I don't miss my ride home," Whitney said. Well, they weren't going to leave without her, but it sounded like a good excuse.

"Oh, I'm sure Samuel won't leave his girlfriend behind. Then he wouldn't be a good boyfriend," Tim replied, not moving and letting Whitney by. "Why don't you sit down and chat a bit with me? Has Sam told you anything about his wonderful older brother?"

From the tone of his voice, she understood it wasn't a question. In fact, there was a slight melody to it. That alone made her pause. Sam said that siren can control day humans with their voice. If she wanted to keep playing the part, she had to do what he asked, even though being near him made every fight or flight sensor inside of her go off.

Whitney sat back down in her seat. She couldn't leave and let Tim be suspicious of why she didn't listen to him.

"My sources say you recently moved to town," Tim said to her. Whitney didn't say anything. If it wasn't a question, she wasn't going to provide information.

Tim must have noticed as he smiled and tried to be friendlier. It didn't matter. She saw in his eyes he was anything but friendly, and from Sam's few comments, everything she suspected was true and probably worse.

"Have you lived in Florida long?"

"Just a year and a half," Whitney replied, looking to the stage and trying to will Sam to appear and see she was cornered by his brother.

"And you must be into music, or is it just musicians?"

Whitney shrugged. That wasn't much of a question either.

"Has Samuel told you he has to go on vacation this weekend?" Tim asked, leaning back like they were old friends chatting.

"He hasn't mentioned anything, but we did just start dating. Not really at the stage of telling each other everything and schedule details to the minute. I think that comes at stage two in the relationship, but once we get there, I'll let you know."

Tim raised an eyebrow to say he wasn't sure if he believed her. "But you are at the stage where you spend lots of quality time alone."

Whitney kept silent again. He could ask any of the sirens how much time they were spending together. She was pretty sure they all knew. Tim didn't need an answer from her.

"Has Samuel told you about having an older brother?" he asked, still trying to gauge her.

Whitney shrugged again in an attempt to make it vague. "He said he had siblings when I mentioned I have a brother."

"I suppose he didn't mention I was older, cuter, and a much better kisser." Tim fake pouted.

He was older, and also drop-dead gorgeous, but she wasn't about to say he was cuter. Sam looked at her with wonder and kindness; Tim looked at her like he wanted to drain her blood. Very big difference. She wasn't about to let that happen. Whitney didn't look back to the stage, but stood up again. She had sat long enough to play his game, even if she didn't know what it was. Just his eyes on her made her want to take a shower. Tim maybe looked like Sam, but he was nothing like him.

"The guys tend to head out quickly after these things. Something about not wanting fans to find out where they live. If they left without you, I can always give you a ride back," Tim offered, this time standing with her.

Whitney knew Sam wouldn't leave without her, but she

had a bad feeling in the pit of her stomach, Tim had done something to try to make that happen. She hurried from the seating gallery and back into the waiting room. As she pulled open the door to leave, she ran right into Sam. He grabbed her arms quickly as he looked over her shoulder, patting her down like she might be missing an arm or two.

"Crazy seeing you here," Tim said as he wandered up behind Whitney. She didn't turn to see his face, but could feel the anger between Sam and Tim, and it wasn't a one-way thing.

"Considering this is my concert, I could say the same to you," Sam told his older brother. He glared at him as he added, "I'd love to stay and talk, but my bandmates are under the impression they need to leave immediately."

Whitney finally saw Tim's face as Sam pulled her to his side.

"I'm guessing you all have a lot of schoolwork to get done. I hear that makes people want to get back home. You know, to study and all." Tim smiled with his sparkling white teeth.

"I'm sure that's it," Sam replied and turned Whitney to the door.

"What, not even a goodbye hug?" Tim called to them. "Oh, yeah. That's not needed since you're coming home this weekend."

Sam didn't turn around and kept nudging Whitney going out the door.

"I prefer you don't head home. It will be much more fun that way."

Tim's last words were muffled as they left the room, but they both still heard him. Under his friendly façade was certainly a threat. Whitney had no idea what she gotten in the middle of, but she was happy there were be a few hours of a bus ride to talk to Sam about it, as long as his friends were busy in the hot tub with the girls they liked to pick up.

CHAPTER 8

Sam stroked Whitney's hair as she slept on his lap. The blonde curls were softer than they looked. It didn't take much to make her pass out in the shower when he fed her. She was hungry, which also makes one very tired. He hoped that would happen as he had a lot of talking to do with his two bandmates, Mark and Leo. They sat across from him on the benches alone since they didn't even pick up girls at the concert like normal, thanks to Tim. Both of them were convinced they needed to leave immediately, and if Sam hadn't commanded them to stay, they would have left him and Whitney behind.

"Bummer. This gig wasn't a coincidence?" Mark asked disappointedly.

It was actually one of the larger ones they had done in a while. The pay was much better and so was their choice in girls. Mark was bummed they hadn't scored any food.

"I had a feeling it wasn't," Sam replied evenly. He was doing his best to keep calm. He needed to talk to the guys without Whitney hearing. "Which one of you was going to tell me that Tim was here?"

Leo looked sheepishly at Mark. Mark stared at the floor of the bus like it was the most interesting thing he had seen all week. Sam needed a different approach. Neither would look him in the eye, and he had a feeling they both knew.

"How long has he been in town?"

Leo met his gaze, confused. "He never left."

Sam ran a hand through his hair. Tim had to have been the mer he was feeling at the pool yesterday when Whitney came by. Sam knew there was someone there watching them, but he figured it was just one of the ones from school, curious about him and Whitney. He didn't think it would be Tim. Tim hated being on land or away from the island. In fact, to know he had been on land for over a day was actually kind of strange. The last time Tim came to land, he made sure everyone knew he was never coming back. Sam would have laughed at him being there if he wasn't there to spy on him.

"I assumed he was here to make sure you go back," Mark added, trying to be helpful.

Sam nodded. That was more than likely why Tim was there. It just stunk that everything with Whitney was happening at the same time. Sam's two friends both looked guilty and ashamed they hadn't said anything. He wasn't about to get mad at them for that.

"Have you hinted that you have to break up with her soon?" Mark asked as he looked at the sleeping Whitney. Sam could see beyond his normal teasing façade, Mark actually cared for Whitney. He was actually the one to hire her at his restaurant.

Sam shrugged. No one would understand if he told them he wasn't going to break up with her, that he couldn't. Then he'd have to explain more than he was willing to say. He just needed to play the part of jerk boyfriend to them, and no one would care.

They knew as little as he did about what Tim was planning. If he knew Tim, he wasn't about to tell anyone. Sam would have to be prepared for anything.

"You guys know there's a new family moving to town," Sam changed the subject.

"As in the kind we'd like to move out of town?" Mark asked, raising an eyebrow in surprise.

He knew exactly what Sam was hinting at and kept it in code in case Whitney woke. They sure couldn't be talking about hunters in front of a day human, and even though she wasn't a day human, Sam still didn't want to scare her any more than she already was. She already wasn't herself after her visit with Tim. He had done his best to be friendly, but Whitney knew better and was rightfully cautious of him.

"Most definitely. I took Whitney down to the beach, and one was coming back on the pathway. He seemed to know his way around, or he was off searching for trouble. We have to keep our eyes open now to make sure no one slips up. With a hunter family hanging around, we're all in danger. And you know where there is one, there is more to come. Shifts will need to be taken to keep the area safe. Tell the rest of the guys we need to meet at my place before school to divvy up the schedule."

The guys both nodded to Sam as he continued to rub Whitney's arm with his thumb while he spoke. He hoped the sirens in town weren't too much to worry about. Everyone on land had been safe since he came to town and implemented his rules. He hadn't actually had someone disobey him in over a year. That wasn't his worry. Whitney was. She was too new at it. If she didn't learn how to fit in better, it was going to be a very big problem. His family would toss her away if she was taken, but he couldn't. Sighing, he rubbed his forehead.

Tim picked the perfect time to start following their dad's order, and it stunk. Not that Sam ever liked him much before, but the way that Tim looked at Whitney made his blood boil. The siren code was to not feed on any day human another had already fed on, but Tim didn't think the code pertained to him. In fact, Tim was one of those sirens that didn't think any of the rules were for him to follow. Tim did as he pleased when he pleased and that wasn't good news for Sam. He had seen how Tim looked at her, and it wasn't just to annoy Sam. This was going to be a long week to get through, and an even longer weekend avoiding his brother. Add into the mix a hunter family moving to town and Sam just felt like he got screwed over with all of it.

He looked over to his two friends, and he could see their worry. They were concerned about the hunter. Any siren in their right mind would be. Hunters had ways to train to be immune to the song of the siren. It didn't bode well for any of the sirens who had never been taught to fight, and that was most of them. They relied too heavily on their voices to get out of everything. Sam's life was overflowing when all he wanted to do was just spend more time alone with Whitney. That wouldn't be an option now. He had to do his job and keep the sirens safe; all of the sirens, including her.

Whitney found that their Tuesday night concert was going to be their last date for a while, and that was more than a little disappointing. At least she still had her Thursday night swim lesson. It gave her one hour alone with Sam, but that was it. While she went to lessons with her questions ready, he whisked her off to the locker rooms to be alone, and those questions really didn't come up. She was more than a little occupied with him, and she figured they could always wait until later. By Friday, she was ready for the weekend and hopefully some time alone with Sam.

"Wait up," Mark called from the closing door of Bingos as she left from her Friday night shift, which went from right after school until closing.

They hadn't seen each other because Sam was busy with "siren stuff" as he put it, but she was busier. Mark had scheduled her for every shift he took that week, and since Sam took most of the swim lessons, Mark had picked up extra shifts at the restaurant, and it seemed that meant Whitney would also. After three nights of working in a row when she only got hired to work two days a week, she was tired and ready to go home to sleep.

Whitney paused outside the door as Mark joined her.

"I'll take you home," he told her, ordering her around very similar to Sam.

Whitney rolled her eyes at him. It had to be a siren trait.

"It's only ten o'clock," she told him. "The murderers

don't like to come out until at least one in the morning, so I have a few hours of safety."

Actually, Whitney didn't fear walking home as she felt the night human blood flow through her. It would be a problem for whatever sorry person tried to hold her up if they did. They wouldn't know what was coming. Sam had explained that sirens didn't train to fight, but they were stronger and faster than day humans. Whitney, though, had been raised a skinwalker and hand-to-hand combat training was part of growing up. With her new senses, strength, and speed, she was more than capable of taking care of herself if someone did try to pull something on her.

"Even so," Mark said, humoring her. "I promised Sam I would take you home. You know he can get a little overprotective."

Whitney rolled her eyes again, but as an order from Sam, Mark probably couldn't say no if he wanted to. If she tried to walk home, he probably gave Mark permission to kidnap her and force her to take the ride home. Yes, Sam was more than a bit overprotective. While she hated to be told what to do, since all she really wanted was sleep, her best course of action was to listen to Mark and take his ride home.

Turning around, Whitney followed him to his car. Like Sam, he drove a nice car but not a new one. They seemed to work that way. Sirens certainly liked finer things in life and from their recording contract could afford them, but they kept things simple and less flashy, probably to draw less attention.

"How are things going with Sam?" Mark asked as Whitney sat down in the car.

She shrugged. What sort of open-ended question was that? Mark was her boss and Sam's friend, but she still didn't know him well enough to talk about Sam with him. And she was more than sure that she didn't want to accidentally say something she would regret.

"Has he told you anything about going home this

weekend?" Mark pried for more information.

"No. Is he going on a trip?" Whitney asked back innocently, knowing full well Sam was avoiding going back at all costs.

Mark drove a minute in silence, looking like he wasn't sure how to proceed.

"I hear you've met his brother," Mark tried to begin the conversation again.

Whitney shrugged again. Oh yeah, she had met Tim, but there was no way she was going to tell Mark what she thought of Sam's evil older brother. Okay. Maybe he wasn't evil, but he wasn't good either. She had looked in his eyes and seen it. His smile was only for show. Why no one else saw that was beyond her. Or maybe they did and didn't care. The little she had learned about the siren, most of them were like Tim, hard, cold, calculating, and uncaring.

"Has Sam told you anything about how traditional his parents are?" Mark kept asking questions as he turned on another road leading her closer to home. Whitney couldn't wait to get out of the car and away from Mark and his questions before she slipped up.

"Aren't all parents a bit old-fashioned?" Yep, just answer a question with an answer. That could keep him going. They were getting close enough to her home.

Mark nodded before adding, "Did he tell you they plan to set up an arranged marriage for him?"

Whitney gave Mark her best pretend shock face. Mark gave her a sad smile and nodded like he bought it.

"I know, nothing against Sam and all, but he's known all along that this weekend he has to go home and probably will have to break up with you," Mark told her, laying a hand on her bare leg.

Genuine shock laced her face, and Mark took that as a sign to continue to comfort her. But her shock wasn't from his words; it was because his touch didn't make her skin tingle like it did when Sam touched her. Here she was thinking it was a siren to siren thing, and as soon as one touched her, they would know. That didn't seem to be the case. Mark was as clueless as ever, and now she had to talk to Sam and ask him what that meant.

"Well, thanks for the warning," Whitney said, slipping out from beneath his hand as she opened her door.

The car hadn't come to a complete stop, but they were at her house, and she didn't want to stay in the car any longer than she had to. She had the very distinct feeling what would come next would include Mark offering to take her out. When she refused, she didn't want to see if he would try to use his siren voice to get her to agree. It wasn't a game she wanted to play and was glad to be out of his car and walking to her home.

Whitney didn't look back, and she raced up to the house and went inside before Mark could follow. Her internal thoughts were debating over whether to tell Sam or not. Something came up with the sirens that was keeping him busy, and maybe it just wasn't the time to tell him about Mark basically hitting on her. Sam hadn't told her what was keeping him when he texted a couple times a night before she worked, but it was because it was siren stuff. He could only tell her the truth when they were certain to be alone. While she had no idea why, she trusted Sam completely. One thing was for sure. He wasn't planning on going back to the island and let his parents marry him off.

Making it to her room, Whitney turned on the light and looked out her window to the driveway. Mark was still sitting there, now on his phone. She waved to him. He nodded and began to back out. Sam was like that, too; always checking to be sure she made it in her house. More than likely he was just acting on Sam's orders, because she was pretty sure the most dangerous thing near her at the moment was Sam's siren friend that looked like he couldn't wait for Sam to be mated off.

Whitney walked over to her phone, which she had left at

home by accident, and turned it on. Sam had texted her a bunch of times. First one said to not go to work. Second was that he realized she was already at work. Third was to let Mark give her a ride home. Fourth was to not go with Mark. Sam was certainly being wishy-washy. The last one said that he would be over at two in the morning to get her, and to have her bags packed. Sam had mentioned that his brother didn't seem to be leaving town, and Sam wanted to keep her safe. Whitney was pretty sure Sam was Tim's target, but she would humor him. A weekend hiding with him didn't sound too bad at all to her.

Sitting down on her bed, Whitney debated taking a shower or not before going to sleep. She constantly felt like there was a coating of grease on her skin when she got home from work. Grease annoyed her. Probably always would since she was a bit obsessive with cleaning, and the slime of grease didn't feel clean.

As she lay on her bed debating if she had enough energy to shower, her phone beeped with another text. Was Sam changing his mind again? Probably. Picking up her phone, she looked at it and saw it was from Trudy. She wanted Whitney to go to school and meet her at the pool. She said Sam was in trouble, and he needed her help. Whitney didn't hesitate as she pulled on a hoodie and her shoes. It would take her more than fifteen minutes to run to the school, but that was all she could do without a car. She was half tempted to call Mark and see if he would come back. He couldn't be too far away, but decided against it. He really creeped her out with all the questioning. Running would have to do.

Whitney left the house without telling her aunt or cousin since neither were home. She'd call them later and straighten it out before either could worry. With the time of night it was, they probably wouldn't check for her until morning or even later, thinking she was sleeping in.

In the dark of the night, with her night human siren vision, Whitney had no problem getting to the school. She kept her pace at a jog in case anyone saw her on her way there but she went as fast as she could without drawing attention to herself. When she finally made it to the school, she looked around the parking lot for Sam's car. It wasn't there, but that didn't mean he wasn't there. Trudy had said he was at the pool.

Whitney continued her jog around to the back gate of the pool. The fence was closed, which was odd because when Sam was there, he never had it closed. The second odd thing was that the lights were off. Yes, Whitney could see fine, but most day humans had bad night vision. Her friends would have left it on for her at least.

Pulling open the gate, she walked forward.

"Trudy," she said quietly. Whitney wasn't sure if anyone was supposed to be at the school, and she didn't want to get her friends in trouble.

She saw that at least a few people were in the water. *What happened?* She crept closer since no one had responded.

Bright lights turned on all around her, momentarily blinding Whitney. She covered her eyes with her hands, but someone grabbed her from behind and ripped her hands from her face, making her squint. Her eyes quickly adjusted as she looked back to the pool. Her friends—Trudy, Tina, Noah, and James—were standing in the water near the deeper end as it was all neck high. From the looks of it, they were fully clothed, but nothing appeared to be holding them in place. Whitney had no clue what was going on.

Straining to get her head around, she didn't need to see her attacker once he spoke.

"I've been following Samuel around all day, but it seems like he wants to play this game of cat and mouse forever. I have plans back home to get to, so I figure this is an easier way."

Tim held her arms twisted behind her so she couldn't move.

"I'm going to call my brother, and you are going to ask him to come here," Tim told her.

"No," Whitney replied. It was exactly what Tim wanted, and it couldn't be good. Tim chuckled making her bounce off his chest as she was pressed against him.

"Let me try this again. You are going to tell my worthless little brother to meet you here." Tim's voice changed, and Whitney heard it.

She didn't want to give anything away, but she was stuck. If she said no, then he would think something was up. If she did what he asked, there was no guarantee he wouldn't do something to her or her friends to get Sam to go with him. The best option was to not reply, which would buy her a little more time.

Whitney looked across the pool to her friends. All she saw in Trudy's eyes was terror. Tina was beside Trudy without her glasses with the same expression on her face. Without the corrective lenses, she looked completely different. If Whitney had seen her on the street, she might not even know it was her friend.

Tim must have taken her silence as agreeing.

"If you try to leave, one of your friends dies," Tim told her as he released her arms. Reaching into her pocket, he pulled out her phone.

Whitney brought her arms back in front of her and rubbed her sore wrists. Because of night human super healing, there wouldn't be a bruise. She looked back to her friends. She couldn't see anything keeping them where they were, and it was four against one. Why weren't they fighting back?

"Time to tell him," Tim told her, offering her the phone.

Whitney glanced at her friends one last time. She didn't want them to get hurt, but she also needed to keep Sam away. His family was nothing but bad news. He'd told her that already a dozen times. She couldn't imagine them actually being like that, but as her friends stood there, she was certain Tim wouldn't hesitate to hurt them. Running wasn't an option. How was she supposed to get out of it this time?

Tentatively, she took the phone that was already dialing Sam's number. Without hesitation, Whitney tossed the phone into the water.

"Oops." She covered her mouth but didn't try to hide how *not* sorry she was.

Tim's face fluctuated from surprise, to anger, to a smile that couldn't mean anything good.

"I have a feeling you're too smart for your own good. What has my brother told you about his family?" Tim's voice had a melody to it.

"That he has jerks for siblings," Whitney spat back at him.

Tim smiled more. "I can see why he likes you. You have the will to defy us and the spunk to back it up. You must really be a fun toy. I'm sorry you met my dear brother first. He must completely bore you." Tim now stood beside her, looking her up and down. "And you must taste delicious."

"Sorry. I don't do that sort of stuff on a first date, or even second or third with someone like you," Whitney replied.

Tim just grinned more. "Oh, how I wish I could sit here all day and play with you, but I don't have time for that. I have to head back home, and I need my little brother to show up. Let's get this game started."

Pulling out his own cell phone, he typed in a number then held it to his ear as he waited for the person to answer.

Whitney glanced back at her friends. 'Are you okay?' she mouthed to them.

Tina couldn't see her clear enough, but Trudy's eyes went wide—like she couldn't answer, even if she wanted to. Then it sunk in. Tim didn't have to tie them up or secure them. They couldn't disobey him.

"Little brother," Tim said into the phone. Then he pulled

it back and huffed. "He sure is in a bad mood," Tim complained. "He hung up on me." His face mirrored sadness that wasn't really there. Tim actually seemed to enjoy the fact that his brother hung up.

Whitney kept her mouth shut as she tried to come up with a plan. Her friends couldn't do anything, and she couldn't leave them behind with Tim. Since she was siren, she could order them to leave. She might be stronger than Tim. She didn't know for sure, though. Sam explained that all blues could order around greens, but they had to follow the higher-ranked siren's command. Since she was pink, he wasn't sure if that made her lower or higher than the blues. Now wasn't the time to try it out, but if she had to, she would.

Tim walked over to her and threw his arm around her shoulder.

"Say cheese," he told her as he held up his phone and snapped a picture. Stepping away, she knew that was the bait to get Sam. She needed to decide what to do quickly.

Tim's phone rang and he grinned. "Oh, hi. Here I thought you might not want to talk to me."

He walked away from the pool a little bit like he was on a leisurely phone call. Whitney decided to see if what she thought was true.

"Can you guys move at all?" Whitney whispered to her friends. They all four looked back at her. "Blink once for no, twice for yes." Trudy stared directly at her and blinked once. She then stared again. "Will he hurt you if I leave?" Whitney still wasn't sure what she was dealing with. Trudy again blinked twice.

Shoot. It was as bad as she thought it would be. She needed to do something. Tim was walking back, still on the phone. Without saying goodbye, he pulled back and hung up on his brother, even though Whitney could still hear Sam's voice coming through the phone.

"He just talks and talks," Tim complained. "Now onto the fun part. My dear brother doesn't want to come home and fulfill his family duty. I think a big part of that is because he found you, and you are just too tempting to leave alone. I mean I wouldn't if I had found you. You are just too much fun. I really wish I'd found you first and saved you from this family drama."

Tim was now standing right next to her as he spoke. Whitney didn't move. Her mind was blanking on what to do.

"Now little Samuel might make a fuss if I don't take you with. He seems pretty attached, and I think I might know why."

With one gigantic shove, Whitney was hurtling toward the water. She wasn't ready to give away that she was a siren—it needed to be her trump card. Using as much energy as she had, she continued to tell her body over and over again that she needed to keep her legs. *I need to keep my legs; fin stay away* was her new chant. She held her breath as she went under the water and kept telling herself to stay human. When she realized that her fin wasn't there, she righted herself and stood up in the water. Good thing Sam had taught her how to swim. She turned to Tim, who was standing on the edge of the pool, and he looked disappointed.

"Well, you're no fun," he complained, sitting down at the side of the pool. "I was sure my brother had turned you, and it would have been perfect. Just showing a day human the mer world is punishable by exile or death. But then I'd have to prove it. Turning you would have made my life much easier."

Whitney stood in the water, her legs itching to be a fin but remaining because she told them to.

"Samuel always wanted to choose his own siren. I was sure he did it to you." Then Tim covered his mouth. "Oh, I get it. He hadn't told you about us yet and planned to do it once he got the chance. I sometimes wish he'd move a little faster. He always has to think so much about what he's doing. Oh well. Guess I get to clean up his loose ends for him."

Tim hopped into the pool and began to wade over to Whitney. She backed up as he came closer. Something inside her said to run as far as she could from him, but she couldn't leave her friends behind.

"Oh, yeah, sorry about all this. I'm sure you have no idea what is going on." Tim tried to sound sympathetic, but wasn't even close.

Whitney made it to the other side of the pool and pulled herself to the edge.

"Oh, what? You don't want to stick around for the show?" Tim turned to her friends. "Turn into your siren form," he ordered them.

Shock registered on Trudy's face as she transformed against her will. Everyone else did, also. Whitney was equally shocked and looked at them. They no longer had their normal hair or eyes. Where Sam changing into a siren left him looking still like himself, her friends were anything but themselves. Trudy's normally red hair was now green to match the long tail she had. Instead of beautiful swirls covering her body, the green scales went up to her neck and down her arms a little. She looked more monster than human in her siren form.

"They are a little scary, aren't they?" Tim said, now beside Whitney. She hadn't noticed he had moved so fast. "I'm sorry your last memories will be of looking at something as grotesque as a green, but what can I do? Loose ends need to be tied up in order for Sam to leave. You four greens have broken siren law by showing a day human your siren side. You are hereby sentenced to death."

"What?" Whitney exclaimed. He had forced them to do it.

Tim grinned at her. "Oh, how sweet. You still care about them even if they are monsters. Did you know that they feed on humans? In fact, the green siren tend to be the most vicious."

"How is that fair? You told them to do it," Whitney proclaimed in defense of her friends who couldn't talk or move.

"Ahh. I know it's unfair. But at least you know they won't be alone," Tim added, reaching up with lightning speed and grabbing her by the neck. "Because any day human that sees us is sentenced to death as well."

With one motion, Tim pulled Whitney into the pool. She didn't have a chance to take a breath before she was plunged into the chlorine water. Water immediately filled her nose and lungs, and she was only minutes away from dying and moments away from being unconscious. Whitney struggled against his grip, but Tim was stronger than her. As she turned, she saw his blue tail swishing in the water beside her. He wasn't going to just kill her; he was going to drain her of blood too. Because she couldn't come up with a solution, her friends were going to die, she was going to die, and Sam would be forced back home to a life he didn't want. Tim was truly the worst brother ever. The only real monster in the pool was him.

The world started to blacken around her. How was it fair that Tim had this much power? He was evil. Everything she had ever been told about night human mers was completely true. They were hideous, evil beings. But she couldn't think about that. She knew better. Sam wasn't evil; he was good. Whitney kept his face in her mind as her body began to shut down. She had failed him.

With one last ounce of effort to hang on, Whitney had enough time to decide to instead let go, expecting to die.

CHAPTER 9

Standing at the edge of the pool, Sam stared at the water. He could feel that Whitney had just been there. He knew she had, and he didn't need to see her phone in the bottom of the pool to confirm it. But she wasn't there now. Where had Tim gone, and where did he take her? Tim had lured him to the pool, and Sam was expecting the worst, but now there was nothing.

When Tim called him, Sam thought that ignoring him and heading back to town was the best option. He led Tim over two hundred miles away, which would give Sam enough time to collect and hide Whitney. Tim's new sudden interest in her was something to worry about. He hadn't expected Tim to do anything yet.

Try as he might, Sam wasn't able to keep Whitney from being a target. He had tried to convince everyone she was just a toy or a new feed, but Tim would see through that. He'd expected that much. But he didn't expect his brother would be at the concert. Sam knew that was the downfall, where he made the mistake of leaving her alone. He should have insisted she stay backstage. Then again, Tim would have found her there. How the heck was Sam supposed to protect the sirens if he couldn't protect his own girlfriend from his brother?

Sam paced the side of the pool. He could tell from the scent that there was more than one mer in the pool. He had to guess, Whitney had been forced to change and possibly the other residue was Tim, but it didn't feel like just Tim. It actually felt like greens. And that was strange. Tim didn't know a single green, nor would he ask them for help. No, that was what blues were for.

"What are you doing out here at this time of night?" Amber asked as she came up the walkway to the pool.

Sam turned to her and tried to come up with a good excuse.

"What are you doing here?" he asked. He had no excuse, and his mind was running wild with worry for Whitney.

"I saw the lights on as I drove by and figured I should check it out," she replied, finally making it to Sam.

Sam didn't reply. It didn't sound like the best excuse, but he didn't have one either that would cover up his worry. It was possible Amber saw something, and it might be worth asking her more.

"Late night swim?" she asked, sweetly, coming up to his side.

Sam wanted to push her away, but let her cling to his arm instead as he thought.

"Nah, one of my swimmers lost their cell phone. See?" He pointed to the pool. That was a good excuse, and at least he thought of it now and not later. It was actually a really good excuse.

Amber pouted.

"Are you really not going back as your father commanded?" She changed the subject expertly, like the cell phone in the pool made her too upset to talk. Amber possibly knew more, and Sam had to keep her talking.

"No. I have to stay here and keep everyone safe," Sam replied.

He had this argument with his father weeks ago, with his brothers, each one that came to talk to him, and every other siren who asked. They were all very shocked and somehow seemed to think that if they kept asking, his choice would change.

"Not all the sirens are heading back, and there's a new hunter family in town."

That had been his argument all along with his father. The greens were still on land. Some would go back if they wanted, but they weren't invited to the party anyway, so most didn't plan to leave. Only the blues were ordered back for the party. If Sam left, then there was no one to defend the greens against the hunters.

"Who cares about the greens? If they follow your rules, they'll be safe. If they can't, then they deserve to be found," Amber replied callously.

"Amber, they are sirens—blue or green. They are still sirens, and my oath was to protect sirens. Not just the blues." He unwrapped his hand from her arm as he walked around the pool. There had to be some sort of clue as to where Tim had taken Whitney.

"Seriously, Sam, seriously?" Amber complained, stomping her feet like a child throwing a temper tantrum.

He didn't look back at her as he looked at the water drops outside the pool. He could see which direction they left. That was a start.

"You care about the greens. You care about your ridiculous day human, but you can't find it in you to care about me."

Sam turned around, not sure how to respond. Amber would never understand about caring and protecting someone else because she could only think of herself. She was exactly what Sam hated in the sirens, and exactly what he had told Whitney about. How he didn't see it sooner was beyond him. He didn't get to time to respond and tell her so before he felt a jolt of electricity run through him.

"Hurry up," she yelled behind her. Several of his friends and fellow blues came out of the shadows with ties to bind him.

"Sorry, man," Leo said as he knelt down beside him. "Your dad gave my parents an order and you know I can't refuse them."

Sam was still unable to move as the shock continued to course through him.

"You're such an idiot, Sam. We would have made a great

pair, and I'm certain that with me beside you, your dad would have chosen you as his heir. Instead, you get to die. Stupid choice. Just to let you know, I'll never forgive you for ruining my life." Amber dropped the stun gun and walked away while the guys finished tying him up.

One point for Tim. Sam would have never thought his friends would turn on him. Now he knew better. All he could hope was that they would take him wherever Whitney was, and he would get the chance to tell her he was sorry he couldn't protect her.

Whitney woke to a strange scent in the air. It was fruity and flowery at the same time. She slowly cracked open her eyes and tried to remember what had just happened. Pulling her hands up to rub her face, her eyes shot open at the realization that she wasn't able to move. She was strapped to a chair with her arms and legs tied tightly.

Whitney looked around frantically and finally realized why she woke. Someone was sitting at her feet, washing them.

"Um, excuse me," Whitney said, interrupting the woman. She glanced up from her spot, and Whitney sucked her breath. The woman's eyes were familiar; they were identical to Sam's in their shape and color. Without a doubt, the lady was a siren.

Quickly, everything rushed back to Whitney. Tim had tricked her into going to the pool. He had tried to get her to lure Sam there, and she had refused. He then tried to kill her, and planned to kill her friends. But what she couldn't understand was why she was alive now. And she knew she was alive because she ached from head to toe.

Whitney looked around the room as the woman stared inquisitively at her. She had no idea where she was. The room had one long cabinet in front of her with a sink and an open window. There were no screens on the window. The cabinets were made of some sort of brown wood and the sink didn't appear to be a normal sink. She could see to one side was more open windows that showed the woods around the building and the other side of the room was a light green wall with nothing on it. Off behind her was a table and more chairs like the one she was tied to, but it still wasn't a place Whitney had ever been. Closing her eyes, she could sense that the ocean was only a walk away.

"My friends. Did Tim kill my friends?" Whitney asked as she opened her eyes and looked back at the woman that was still watching her.

Wrinkles formed in the woman's forehead. She didn't seem to know what Whitney was asking.

"I had four friends that Tim had ordered into the pool. He made them change and said that they would be sentenced to death. Did he kill them?"

Whitney didn't expect her to answer, but was hoping the lady's face would give it away. If this woman was one of Sam's relatives, she was sure they wouldn't give her information. They had to be related to Tim also, and were probably doing exactly what he asked. She had to hope there would be enough in the other woman's expression to tell her what had happened to everyone.

"Do you mean the greens?" the woman finally asked, her voice soft and barely audible.

"Yeah, I suppose." Whitney remembered seeing their fins were green and the scales that covered most of their bodies were also green, but to her, they weren't just "greens". They were her friends.

"Timothy was going to punish them, but since they broke no laws, they remained in town when he brought you here," she explained, reaching for something before turning back to Whitney's feet.

The stench hit her first as the woman poured a new liquid on her cloth. First, she felt a bit of fear and worried that the woman was going to use the foul-smelling stuff to hurt her, but soon enough Whitney wrinkled her nose and really wished her arms were free to itch it. So far the smell of the stuff was the worst part of it. Nothing stung as the lady worked more on cleaning her.

"What are you guys going to do with me?" Whitney asked. The woman seemed friendly enough and answered her first question. Maybe she would talk more. Whitney needed answers to form some sort of plan. She wasn't just going to sit and do what the sirens wanted as clearly what they wanted wasn't anything close to what she did.

The woman began to rub Whitney's toes with the awful-smelling stuff. It was cold but didn't sting, so that was a relief. It seemed it wasn't something to hurt her.

"I've been ordered to clean you to be presented to the king," the woman replied as she worked. Soon enough she moved to Whitney's other foot with the stinky stuff.

Whitney glanced at the foot the woman had been rubbing. Her bright pink toenail polish was gone. Whitney sighed. She had just put that on two days ago, and it was perfect. She was getting good at doing her nails; she wasn't embarrassed to wear flip flops with everything now. When she had first moved to Florida, she realized how much better people had their finger and toe nails done. She couldn't afford a manicure or a pedicure, so she had to practice time and time again to get it done well.

"Does the king have something against dirty feet?" Whitney asked, trying to keep the conversation going. She wanted to know as much as she could. It didn't seem like there was going to be a way out of it, but that didn't mean she had to go down without a fight.

"No," the lady replied as she worked. Soon enough she was done with the second food.

Whitney sighed. All that hard work painting her nails had been for nothing. The woman went back to the first foot to be sure it was perfectly cleaned.

Whitney waited a second. Would the strange siren say

anything more?

Nope… and Whitney didn't have the patience to wait.

"Then you just like to clean feet?"

The woman stood up and walked away from Whitney to the sink without a word, but she gave a small smile. She dumped out the bad-smelling stuff and refilled the bowl, pouring something much better smelling into it as she did so. Returning to Whitney, she continued to wash her feet again.

"Has my son not taught you anything about being a siren?" she asked in her same soft voice.

Shock was all Whitney felt as she stared. The lady was older, but not much. She didn't look a day or two past thirty, and certainly not old enough to be an eighteen-year-old's mother, let alone a mom to anyone older than that, like his twenty-something siblings.

The lady rubbed the better-smelling stuff on Whitney's feet before going up her calf muscle also. When both feet were clean and smelling as wonderful as the air around them, the lady returned to the sink to dump everything out. Whitney found her voice again.

"You're Sam's mom?" she asked in disbelief.

After the lady rinsed out the bowl and turned it upside down on the edge of the sink, she wiped her hands on a towel.

"Yes, Samuel is my son," she replied, turning to Whitney with those eerily similar eyes.

"But you can't be old enough to have that many children," she added. Sam's family was huge.

The lady laughed. "I'm plenty old enough to have a young man as a son. And he's my only son. Sam's siblings are his half brothers and sisters."

"Oh," was the only response Whitney could come up with. She hadn't thought of that.

"I'm the king's fifth wife, Queen Mira," the lady continued. "And I wish I were meeting you under different circumstances. From how angry Timothy has been, I'm guessing you're really important to my son. Timothy doesn't want anything unless Sam wants it, also."

"Wait. Sam's a prince, like literally a prince?" Whitney asked as she finally realized what it meant when his mother said she was wife to the king. Her friends didn't call Sam "Prince Sam" because he bossed people around like she thought. It was because he really was a prince.

The lady who had been washing her feet, a queen at that, just smiled.

"Sam's never really been one for titles. I'm glad to see that didn't change when he went landside."

Whitney still stared at her in awe. The queen pulled up a chair across from Whitney and sat, gazing at her.

"Samuel seems to have left out a lot about the mer world," she began, looking Whitney over. "Like once you reach eighteen, you age at a quarter of the pace of day humans."

Whitney searched her mind. It wasn't like Sam didn't try teaching her, it was just that he started with her least favorite subject, history, which in turn made her tune him out a little bit. Okay, a lot.

"That's one of the main reasons sirens return to the island in their early twenties, because people realize they aren't aging. It also makes you stand out for hunters."

That made a lot of sense. Sam never mentioned any older sirens and had said several were heading back after graduation. It now seemed like most of them headed back quicker than she imagined. How much more had she missed from his first lesson? It was her fault for not listening, and also for not asking more questions. They had spent the last night together after school, but they didn't spend it talking. That would have been a bit more helpful.

"So the whole washing me thing …" Whitney began to ask, coming out of her surprise finally. Beautiful auburn eyes stared intently at her. "If I'm going to die like Tim wants, why wash my feet? Sorry if I offend you, but it seems a bit odd."

The queen laughed, it was almost a very quiet twinkling-like noise, very melodic.

"I can't imagine how strange this must be for you. Yes. I'm sure Tim wanted to kill you."

Wanted? He tried, Whitney thought, but she didn't add it to the conversation.

"But he isn't in charge and might have had a change of heart. My husband will decide what to do with you based on where you fall in the siren world. Normally you would be killed for knowing about us, but since you are siren that makes thing complicated. There's a lot of politics involved." She left her answer open-ended.

"Yeah, Sam tried to explain all of that to me, too. It didn't really take." Politics was her second least favorite subject.

"I now see why Tim went to his father, asking for you to be his mate. You have quite a bit of spunk to you. I'm sure that's something Sam saw right away, too, and something Tim would miss because you were just a day human." The queen sat in her chair, her back straight and appearing very regal now as she talked.

Whitney's mouth dropped open. "His mate? First, he tries to kill me, and then wants to marry me? How crazy does he think I am? No way I would agree to that. Tim wouldn't be a choice for my mate if he was the last living person on the planet. Yeah… That's never going to happen."

The queen gave her a pitying smile. "You have no one to claim you as their family. The king is the one who decides what will work best for you," she replied, like she knew exactly what that meant. Whitney wondered if there was more behind her words. The queen didn't elaborate, and Whitney didn't feel it was quite her place to ask more.

"How does the king decide where I belong and if I live?" Maybe that was a question she could answer.

The queen gave a little shrug. "He wants to see your fin

again. When you were brought in, it was pink, but since siren are blue and green, we needed to get you cleaned to find out what color your fin really is."

"Cleaned. Yep, you confused me again." Whitney really wished her hands were free as her nose itched, and she wiggled it a bit.

"I really need to scold my son. Not only did he forget to tell you normal stuff, he forgot to tell you even the basics about the sirens and transforming." She shook her head with a sad smile. "When you transform you know that your clothing doesn't disappear, right?"

Whitney nodded and then got the idea to bend down to get that itch. She could just make it to her finger and successfully scratched her nose.

"If you were a blue and you were wearing bright red pants, your fin would be slightly purple in color."

Whitney shot back up. "What?" Sam had never mentioned that.

The queen shook her head again, obviously disappointed with her son.

"The clothing you wear kinds of melts into you as you transform. It can affect your fin color. We were a bit concerned that your choice of clothing color to wear and your toenail polish affected your fin color strongly because you're new. How new are you?"

Whitney stared at her, and for once, realized that she wasn't sure what sorts of things she should say. Sam had said that his parents tried to throw him away when he was a kid by placing him across the US in a different ocean. What should she say to someone that might not actually like her son much?

"Is Sam safe?" she asked, not answering the question before her.

The queen appeared to be thrown off, and she quickly tried to hide her emotion behind a neutral mask, but there was enough for Whitney to see that she was sad.

"For his crimes, Sam will be put on trial before the king when the moon is high in the sky," the queen replied. "And punishment will be immediate."

Whitney stared hard at the woman. There was much she didn't know or understand, and there was no time to learn it. Sam had tried to teach her, but there was much to catch up on. And since Tim now asked for her as his mate is was all beyond belief. She couldn't tell if Sam's mother cared, but she couldn't chance it. If they had Sam, then Whitney needed a plan. She wasn't going to let him be punished for saving her life. All she needed was to figure out how to get out of the restraints, find Sam, and make a break for it. Not that difficult … or at least she hoped not.

The queen left Whitney alone when she refused to give more answers. Whitney just couldn't share much more because she wasn't sure if her answers would get Sam in more trouble. At least it seemed like the queen pushed it all off due to ignorance and easily gave up, instead of knowing that Whitney was actually refusing. Unfortunately, she didn't untie her before she left. That would have made things easier. Whitney was left alone but still unable to do anything. Her view outside of the place wasn't much, either. The windows faced the woods.

Alone in the room, Whitney finally looked around again. She was certainly in some sort of kitchen, she saw the sink and some dishes beside it after all, but it wasn't much of a kitchen. It consisted of one long cabinet with four doors and a sink in the middle. That was it. Whitney turned to each side and tried to see more around her. There was a window on her right side about ten feet away, but even if she hopped her chair over there, she wouldn't be able to see out. It was too high up on the wall. She could only see pretty blue skies and treetops. Everything she could see in the room gave it a very island feel with teak cabinets and tile floor, but it still didn't give her an ounce of information as to where she was or how to get home.

Whitney attempted to look behind herself to see what else was in the room, but she had been positioned closest to the sink, so there wasn't much to see. As she twisted her head left, she could make out a doorway. She really wanted to know where it led. Was she in a house, an apartment, or what? Was the queen nearby, or was someone guarding her? They obviously didn't trust her, since they had tied her up in a chair, but for now it seemed like she was alone.

Sitting perfectly still, Whitney listened for any sound at all. Was she truly alone?

A bird sat outside the window, occasionally tweeting, but that was all the noise she could hear. There was no other breathing in the room, no other shuffling of feet, nothing else to hear. It was like she was in a sound-proof kitchen.

If she was truly alone, she needed to try to leave. She didn't want to sit around and wait for some king, one that would rather get rid of his youngest son than accept him, to decide her fate. And she certainly wasn't sticking around to mate with Tim. She had looked in his eyes and knew his type. There was no compassion of any sort in that guy. He was rotten right down to the core, and she understood that very well since he didn't hesitate to try to kill her in the swimming pool. Sam had explained, more than once, that the sirens didn't look at day humans as anything but food, but to kill her without reason other than to upset his brother just seemed ridiculous … until she found herself underwater.

She needed to break free. That was step number one. Figure out where she was and where she would go would have to come next, but no need to worry about something like that if she couldn't get free. Her first attempt was to try to move the chair. It was solid, or at least weighed enough with how she was tied to it. She wasn't going to be able to break the arms or legs off it to get free. Darn sirens used sturdy materials for chairs.

The plan to break free would have been easier if being a siren came with Superman strength. She was stronger than a normal human, but not strong enough to break the heavily braided ropes. Then again, they wouldn't have left her alone tied down if she could. They already knew she was a siren too. Magical powers would have been nice, also. Then she could just disappear and magically transport herself home. Nope, that wasn't an option either. But she did have cool transforming powers that took her clothing with her. Whitney glanced at her arms. The ropes tying her were tight. Were they tight enough to be considered clothing if she transformed? She had never purposely turned into a siren, but if she could control her legs going fishy now, couldn't she do the reverse?

Whitney stared hard at the ropes. She had to hope and try.

Without being completely sure, Whitney attempted to will herself some fins. Nothing happened, so she closed her eyes and tried to create a mental picture of it, hoping that would be what she needed. After a few more moments, she opened her eyes and still wasn't a mermaid. That was unfair. She wanted it to be easy. Maybe if she pictured water instead. She closed her eyes a second time and thought of Victoria Falls. She'd seen a documentary in school about the great waterfall. Now that was water. Peeking through one eye was enough to see it didn't do a thing. It wasn't like the rest of her escape would be easy either, but it would give her the confidence to do it if she could only get out of the chair she was tied to.

Whitney twisted in her chair again. If she wasn't going to be able to use her siren half to get out, then she would use her own day human wiles instead. There was no way she was going to just sit around and wait. Searching the room, she continued to look for something sharp enough to cut the ropes on her wrists. Could she do it even if she found something sharp? She'd seen it done on TV shows; she had to try. She grinned as there was a cupboard drawer open just enough to see the silver glint of silverware inside. *Jackpot.*

Shuffling her chair as much as she could, Whitney tried to make it the five feet to the sink cupboard. It took a lot of effort just to move the chair. It was way more solid than she first thought. She shuffled it more, going only centimeters at a time. *Shuffle. Shuffle. Shuffle. Catch her breath.* She worked out her own rhythm, getting closer and closer. *Shuffle. Shuffle. Stop.*

Suddenly, she heard a door opening and froze in place. Was someone coming back to check on her?

Remaining still, Whitney silently cursed herself for not turning the chair around in the process of trying to move it. Her whole situation would be better if she could see what was going on behind her. Well, it wouldn't be better, considering that would take being free and back home in bed. She had a major headache—probably from almost drowning. That always gave her a headache.

Quick, soft steps padded around to the front of her. Some guy hastily bent down and cut through the ties on her hands. She had no idea who he was, but since he was freeing her, she wasn't about to complain. The guy cut the ropes on her legs also.

"Why?" Whitney asked, causing the guy to glance up as he cut the last one.

"Because mermaid hair is impossible to break and stops you from transforming."

Whitney looked at the young man. That wasn't really the answer she was seeking. It was a great fact to know, but she wanted to know why he was helping her. He seemed to notice her confusion.

"Um, because we're friends, and my sister would kill me if they did anything to harm you," he replied.

Whitney did a double take. She knew who he was once he said "friends."

Noah finished cutting her free. "And there's the small matter that I promised Prince Sam, also. And I can't go back on a promise to him. He's the only reason we're all still alive. If he hadn't turned you, Tim would have killed all four of us for showing you that we're siren," Noah finished explaining as he stood up and offered her a hand.

Whitney stared at him. Like his twin sister, without his glasses, he was barely recognizable.

"You have to get out of here. When night comes, they'll start Sam's trial, and they will bring you with to show what he did. If you're gone, they'll have to take Tim's word. Without you, they can't kill Sam for him turning you since the evidence is gone," Noah explained quickly.

"He'll be free?" Whitney asked, as this wonderful plan seemed to plop into her lap.

"Not exactly, and neither will you. Sam left you this. He said there's enough money for you to go home and hide away," Noah replied, pulling Whitney in the direction of the part of the room she couldn't see before.

Whitney planted her feet. "What will happen to him?"

Noah shrugged, not meeting her eyes. Even though he looked different, she knew Noah. He was trying to not tell her. Just like the other sirens she knew. It was their normal reaction when they didn't want you to know something.

"What are you leaving out?" She gave him a direct question he couldn't avoid.

"Sam will never be free again," he explained. "He will never be allowed to leave the island for land. If a siren is even suspected of doing the things Tim will accuse him of, then Sam is a liability. He will have to stay here forever."

Whitney took in a breath. He talked much of how he hated the island and never wanted to go back. Now he was trapped there, all because he saved her life.

"They can't do that to him if I leave. You said I'm the evidence," Whitney complained. It wasn't fair. If it was his word against Tim's, then why would they just believe Tim?

"Telling day humans about the night human world is a crime punishable by death. They don't have a punishment for turning someone into a mer. Without you to testify against him—that he told you about night humans—then his only confirmed crime will be that he turned you, which can only be proven by words. They can't do any sort of extreme punishment without physically having you. He said if you go home to your brother, you will be protected."

Whitney knew that was true. She wasn't a skinwalker anymore, but she was still family. If she went back there, they would protect her. The skinwalkers were very territorial, and they would never let the siren come in and take her. Sam was right about that.

"Take this, and I'll lead you to the ocean. Land is straight to the west, just keep the sun at your back, and you'll be there in no time," Noah explained, turning to leave and pulling her with him.

"Wait," Whitney said. She wasn't comfortable with leaving Sam behind. If he came with her, she was sure her family would protect him also. "Sam can't be found guilty of telling me about night humans because I used to be one."

Noah froze in his tracks.

"What?" His eyes were wide as he turned around.

"I used to be a skinwalker. Sam thinks that's why, when he just tried to save me from drowning, he turned me instead. He can't be found guilty of telling me anything about night humans. I already had heard of sirens and mermaids before."

Noah faltered as he tried to turn back to lead her out of the house. That changed everything. Her knowledge was key to setting Sam free.

"Sam knew this?" Noah asked as they walked through a small living room.

"Yes," Whitney replied, wanting to look around but focusing on her friend. She needed to see what else she was missing. Obviously, her admission meant something to Noah, but Sam not using it also meant something.

"Then we still need to get you out of here. If he knows

and still is sending you away, then he has a reason. He wants you to be safe." Noah reached for the door, and Whitney stopped. "We need to do what he asks. He knows this world better than both of us. We need to keep you safe."

Yes, it was true that Sam wanted her safe—and he was risking her friend to do so—but she couldn't just leave him. It wasn't because of his great kissing or her massive crush on him, either. It was because he was a good guy. He didn't deserve any sort of punishment for being who he was. And the sirens on land needed him. Heck, she hadn't seen him all week, and that wasn't by choice. He was keeping them all safe. He was dedicated to them. She needed him back on land, and the sirens needed him. Sam couldn't stay on the island forever. She wouldn't allow it.

Whitney sat down in the nearest chair. She couldn't leave him. She could never tell him the real reason why, but she knew it in her heart. She loved him.

CHAPTER 10

Sam didn't even try to escape. His fate was sealed the moment he saved Whitney, and he knew it. The funny part was even after his father yelled at him, he would have never done it any other way. He had as much power to *not* save Whitney as he did to make the sky rain. From the first moment he met her, he was done. He couldn't get her out of his mind. Every free moment, she was all he could think of. That blonde-haired, blue-eyed beauty flew into his life like a tornado, turning everything around and nothing was the same afterward. And he was fine with it. In fact, he was more than fine. He wished he had the chance to see her one last time before she escaped to tell her thank you. She had changed his life, and it was worth it. Every moment he had with her in the past week was worth everything he'd have to go through and would have to last a lifetime. His punishment was coming, and there was no getting out of it.

Growing up in the siren world was hard, but it was worse if you didn't fit in. All around him, the sirens considered themselves superior to all the mer. And, yes, in many ways they were. But that didn't mean they needed to treat everyone like second-class citizens. It was even worse to be raised in the royal family. They felt they were at the top of the food chain, and there wasn't a day that went by that Tim didn't remind Sam he needed to force everyone to follow his will. It was a wonder Sam turned out normal with what he had to deal with every moment of his childhood. Tim was one of the nicer of his siblings.

Sam had resented his father for years for sending him out young, but it was a blessing. He was able to get away and find his own way in the world. The freedom had been great, but the past year was even better.

Punishment would come when the moon was fully up in the sky above the island. Sam looked out the window of his mother's home. It wouldn't be much longer. He hoped that Whitney had made her way far enough away that no one would find her. Noah would make sure she got out. He wasn't a bad siren, and he seemed to like Whitney, even when he thought she was a normal day human.

Sam made another loop around the room as he paced. By the time he left, there would be lines from where he walked. His mother wouldn't mind, but he wanted to see how his perfect father would take it. Sam stopped as someone walked up the pathway to the front door. When he saw who it was, he continued walking.

"Still mad at me?" Amber asked as she strode past the two sirens keeping watch of the door.

It was pretty pathetic there was only two. Sam could easily get by two men. But his father trusted he wouldn't do anything that would endanger Whitney. And he was right. Until he knew she was safe, Sam would wait in the house.

Sam raised one eyebrow at Amber. Mad? Furious was more like it. Amber had been his friend since they were little. He trusted her and even after she began to show a jealous streak, he still trusted her. Now that was gone. He was pretty sure she set Whitney up with Tim. No one else would have told his family about him dating a human.

"Hey, you're the one that got yourself into this." She raised her hands like she was surrendering. "I was just trying to protect you."

Sam still didn't reply. He had never seen anything but a younger sister in Amber, but that was obviously not how she viewed him. Protecting him didn't seem like the right word for what happened. Amber grabbed his arm to keep him from pacing.

"Honestly, Sam. I didn't think you'd turned her. Now you're facing possible death for that." Amber chided him like a child, or better yet, like a disobedient boyfriend—something he was never going to be for her.

Yanking his arm away, he moved as far across the room as he could so that he didn't end up facing a second charge of hurting another siren. He wasn't one to hit a girl. His mother had raised him with manners, but Amber was pushing him to his breaking point. First, she helped his brother take his girlfriend and then she helped kidnap him to bring him back to the island. There was nothing in that behavior that said she was acting as a friend. Everything she did was to get back at Whitney for being what Amber wanted to be. And the fact that she acted like everything was going to get better was grating on his last nerve.

"I thought she was just a toy. You said that to everyone. I figured once your toy was dead, you'd come home and behave like you were supposed to." Amber pouted. Her arms were crossed, like she was attempting to enhance her chest, still trying to get him to fall for her.

"Amber," Sam said quietly, "it was never going to be you." He enunciated each word to be sure she understood.

Her face visibly dropped before she could hide her reaction.

"There isn't a single mer on the island I would have agreed to bond to. I would rather have been cast out alone the rest of my life than bond to someone I don't love. It wasn't and will never be you. Even if my father tells me I have to mate with you, I'd choose exile over that. Heck, at this point I'd choose death. Do you understand? No matter what happens to Whitney, it will never be you." He hadn't meant to sound mean, but she was getting to him, and he never seemed to be able to get through to her. Maybe if he had, she wouldn't have brought Whitney into this. It was his fault that Whitney was involved.

Now Amber looked shaken. She must not have thought of that option. Amber's shock melted into anger.

"You messed everything up, and I hope you pay for it.

I'm ten times the siren she could ever be. You're the one that will regret not choosing me when you had the chance. I hope you get everything you deserve." She turned on her heels and marched back out of the room.

Sam shrugged as the two guards looked baffled by her actions. He was only telling her the things he hadn't told anyone before. He could understand that it upset her, but it didn't change anything. There was no way he would regret not choosing her. He never wanted her in the first place. And by now it didn't matter. He was going to be confined to the island forever. To live a boring life in a boring place. But at least Whitney would be free. That he could live with.

Finally, Sam sat down. There was no need to wear himself out. He had set everything up as best he could and protected her. Her life would go on, and he would live knowing that he did everything in his power to do that. There was no going back and doing it over. He had done what he could. He could face his father and the siren. He was more than ready.

Leaning back in the chair, Sam closed his eyes. There were many regrets in his life, but only one he was sad about. He pictured Whitney and smiled. He never got to tell her that he loved her, but that was okay. He showed her that by freeing her. She would know that. Even though he wished he could see her again, it was best this way.

"Little brother, ready to go?" Tim asked from the doorway.

Sam didn't open his eyes, but let the last little bit of Whitney's sparkle keep him going. He would be strong for her and accept his fate like he was meant to. Standing up, he looked at his brother. Tim was grinning ear to ear while he waited. Sam followed as Tim led him out of the house.

"Do you want to know something?" Tim asked, acting like he was actually happy about something.

"No," Sam replied. Anything that made Tim happy wasn't worth knowing.

"I asked Dad if I could have her," Tim replied, completely ignoring Sam.

Sam shrugged. Whatever girl he was asking for would be his regardless. Not many sirens could refuse Tim. He was one of the stronger ones. Last year when Tim turned eighteen, he had asked to wait on choosing a mate because he still needed to shop around. Their father had agreed, and Tim had dated a new girl every week. Sam really didn't care which one he had chosen.

"Good for you," Sam replied with fake cheer.

Leading him farther down the dirt path and closer to the ocean, Tim continued to grin. Sam felt bad for whatever girl he had chosen. While Tim was attractive and came from the royal family, the only thing that was royal about him was that he was a royal pain.

"Do you want to see who I chose?" Tim asked, as they started to get near the meeting amphitheater where the sirens would be gathered to see the spectacle that was his trial.

"No," Sam replied.

"Oh, I think you do," Tim added in a sing-song, teasing voice. Tim was in a really good mood, but Sam knew that it was probably not just the girl he chose, but also because Tim would get to see him punished. Tim loved the exhibition of a trial and getting to play the main role in the accusing game would be a cherry on the top.

Sam walked by Tim and continued down the pathway to the amphitheater which was situated beside the ocean. Tim hurried to catch up and pushed Sam off the path, onto a much smaller second path that led behind the stage. Sam didn't try to go back to the first path. He didn't want to see the poor girl Tim was going to mate to, but this way he didn't have to walk past all the eyes of the people sitting there, judging him silently. Sirens were wonderful at casting judgment, especially since they were all power hungry. One more person thrown off the hill would make it easier for them to climb.

Climbing down the rock stairs, Sam followed Tim around the back of the seating area. Tim stayed in front of him the whole time, blocking his view as they rounded the corner. Sam bumped into him as he suddenly stopped. He spun around and smiled, not sweetly, more vindictively.

"I asked father if I could have her as a mate."

Tim pointed to a glass bowl that was large enough to hold a mer. Sam's heart sank. Whitney was sitting in the bowl with her bright pink fin on display; arms crossed as she stared daggers at Tim.

Whitney glared at Tim as he stood there. He had had fun stripping her clothing off before throwing her into the glass bowl. How they had a glass bowl big enough to fit a person was beyond her. Now she sat in the water, feeling a bit like a goldfish as Tim appeared before her again. She had already tried to get out, and the perfectly round sides were impossible to climb with a fin. Tim was now back, and if she could get close enough, she wasn't going to hold back as she smacked him. Maybe if she put some siren strength behind it, she could actually hurt him. If that didn't work, she could always kick him between the legs. Day or night human, that was bound to hurt.

As Tim turned around, Whitney caught a glance of a head of dark hair that made her heart beat fast. Her anger instantly disappeared as she stared at Sam. He stood there in shock.

Sam ran over to the bowl, but Tim caught him just before he could reach it. Sam bucked him off, turning to take a swing at Tim, but stopped as soon as a regal-looking man walked between them. Whitney had no clue where she was and really had no clue who the man was, or where he came from. They were close to the ocean, she heard its song, but she couldn't see it. In fact, all she saw were some trees and large stones that shot up into the dark night sky.

"There will be no fighting before we get through this

night," the man stated, looking at both Sam and Tim as he spoke, his voice scolding while still soft.

"She's not a part of this," Sam said through clenched teeth.

"You're correct that she isn't on trial for what you did, but we will still need to decide what to do with her," the man replied.

"But, Father," Sam started to complain. That made it clear to Whitney who the older man was.

The king beside Sam didn't look like a father to over a dozen children; he looked like the oldest brother. Maybe he could pass for forty at the oldest; his slight beard made him look older, but even that could be a stretch. The man glared at Sam in some sort of silent warning, causing Sam to turn on his heels and walk away. Tim grinned and followed him. Both brothers were gone.

"You've caused quite the stir," the king said to Whitney as he turned back around to face her. "It seems like both my sons are very interested in you."

Whitney knew this was her time. She needed to make sure the king knew the truth, and Sam wouldn't be killed because of what he did.

"Sam didn't break the law in telling a day human about night humans. I already knew about night humans," she blurted out before he could interrupt her.

The king rubbed his beard. He looked nothing like the calloused man that Sam refused to respect and return home to. In fact, she didn't see the malice of someone who hated his son like she expected. The king stared at her through the clear glass, stroking his chin more.

"All my sources say you were a day human. There are only one set of day humans I know that know about night humans. If Sam changed a hunter into one of us, that's a more serious crime you are admitting to."

Whitney quickly shook her head to shake off the shock of the accusation and to try to get him to understand that she really wasn't that.

"I'm not a hunter. I promise you that. And yes, I was a day human before, but that was because a witch took my night human out of me. I grew up as a skinwalker. I was a cougar," Whitney quickly explained, thankful that the king was taking the time to listen and not jump to conclusions.

The king stared hard at her, as if he was trying to see if she were telling the truth or not.

"My parents were murdered when my night human was taken from me. I was sent to live with my aunt because I'm not a night human now. *Really.* Sam didn't tell me about night humans or even about sirens. I had learned about all the different kinds growing up since I was one. I've known about them since before I was able to talk. He didn't break that law."

The king still stared at Whitney, and it was a bit unnerving. He didn't show any indication either way if he believed her or not. Whitney wanted to plead more, but someone came around the nearest rock.

"They are ready for you, dear," the queen told the king

"Aren't they always," he teased back as he offered her an arm and walked away without another word. Whitney was left without knowing what the king thought, or if she had swayed him.

As soon as she was left alone, Noah came out from his hiding spot.

"Are you sure you want to do this?" he asked.

Whitney shrugged. "It's a little late now. I can't seem to get my feet back, so I'm kind of stuck in the bowl."

Noah shook his head. "We are going to have to teach you all this stuff. The bowl is made to hold mer, even strong ones like Sam can't get out of there, so don't feel like it's you. The water has healing stuff in it. It makes you remain a siren so you can't just climb out."

"Kind of like the siren hair ropes?" Whitney asked.

Yes, she needed to be taught more about the siren world,

but there wasn't time for that now.

"Did he look like he believed you?" Noah asked, still glancing around like they would be caught.

"I don't know," Whitney replied. She truly didn't. The king was an impossible person to read.

"Then let me go get a ladder and get you out of there. I only agreed to this because you had a point to make." Noah was scanning the empty area, obviously plotting her escape.

"Noah. You did what I asked. None of this is your fault. I asked to be here, and I'm not leaving until I see that Sam is treated fairly. I'm not going to run away from this," she explained for the tenth time. She was beginning to understand that the greens weren't as strong as the blues, and running was their preferred style.

"And what if they make you bind to Tim? What then? Not only will Sam be trapped here forever, he'll have to live seeing you as Tim's property."

Whitney made a gagging noise as she pretended to puke. "No way possible I'll bind to him."

"Sometimes you don't have a choice," Noah replied.

"Actually, with that sort of thing you do," Whitney replied. She had been a night human long enough to know what binding to someone meant. It was a choice. You had to love them to do it.

"What if the king orders it? I've seen him do it. He's a siren, and the most powerful one at that. If he tells you that you love the person and will bind to them, then you will." Noah sounded like he spoke from experience.

"No one can tell me who to love." Of that Whitney was sure. Not even the king, no matter how powerful.

"They'll be back soon. Are you sure you don't want me to get you out of there so you can make a break for it?"

"No. I'm not going anywhere," Whitney replied, set on seeing it through. She wasn't going to let Sam do this alone. She would be there with him, letting him know that much. He was probably going to be mad, but oh well. It was her life, and she was pretty stubborn.

Water sloshed around as two very large siren carried her glass bowl around the large rock that was the direction Sam had gone. As soon as they made it past, Whitney could see what she had been missing now from her prime seat. There was an amphitheater with over a hundred faces staring back. Right near the front, Tim sat and grinned as Whitney was brought in. Sitting on the stage was the king in a stately-looking stone throne with Sam's mother beside him. Sam was in front of his father on his knees, head to the ground, but he looked up as soon as Whitney was brought in. She had the perfect seat in her glass bowl as it was left on the stage, prominently displayed for all those there to view.

They all gaped at her in shock. They were used to a two-level system of blues and greens, but they looked at her as if she had a third head, not a different color tail. Whitney stared back at all the confused faces. She didn't blame Sam one bit for wanting to leave all these people behind.

Whitney continued to stare at the siren watching at her as she realized something odd. They all looked back with blue eyes—crystal blue eyes. She didn't have a blue or green tail and she lacked the blue eyes they all had too. Too bad it wasn't the time for questions, because that was just one more thing added to her list to ask Sam when she got the chance. With him kneeling before his father, she hoped she would get the opportunity.

"As we can all see, you have turned a day human into a siren, and we must punish you," his father said as soon as the staring and chattering died down a little bit.

Whitney wanted to defend Sam, and he must have sensed it as he looked up at his father.

"I take full responsibility for my actions," Sam stated.

Surprise shone from the older man's eyes, and Tim's smile actually faltered.

"Whitney was, in fact, a day human when I met her. I was assigned with teaching her how to swim. Under my guidance, she did learn how to swim, but I failed. I let her almost drown."

Whitney watched him and had no idea what was going on. The fact that Sam was speaking surprised everyone, but even as he spoke there was more astonishment. Maybe they expected him to defend himself, but instead, he was confirming that he broke their law.

"I couldn't let her die. The hunters are always around looking for suspicious drownings. I used my blood to save her. At the time I didn't know she had been a night human previously, and I surely didn't know it would turn her. But it did, and I'm prepared to face the consequences."

Whitney's mouth hung open in confusion along with the rest of them. He was confessing.

"All I ask is that you let her go free. She didn't ask to be part of the sirens, and she isn't bound to our laws. Even her tail agrees with that." Sam smiled over at her, and she felt her heart race. He was taking full blame to get her off the island.

The king stared at Sam without saying a word. The people in the audience began to mumble to their neighbors, and soon it was loud enough that Whitney was distracted as she was trying to hear from one conversation to another. She wasn't sure if the audience held sway over the king but she wanted to hear what they said. Whitney glanced over everyone. They were all just as confused as she was except for Tim. He was scowling. He obviously didn't like Sam's speech.

"Son, you've pointed out a very odd fact," his father said quietly, and the people instantly hushed. "A fact that you didn't tell me before, one that the girl has also mentioned."

Sam looked at his father questioningly, and a flicker of sadness came over his features.

"It seems I can't grant your request of letting her go free

when, in fact, she knows of night humans. Then she must also know that the night humans don't like the sirens, and we shouldn't exist. We cannot allow her to be on her own. She's a liability. If she were to be found, they would come looking for us all."

Sam rubbed his hands down his face. His last attempt to free Whitney wasn't working as he wanted it. She gave him a sad smile in return for his quick glance. He had tried, and she understood that. All she could hope now was that they wouldn't hurt him.

"And there is the fact of the tail. I don't know exactly what it means, but it might mean that she needs to die. We have an order in our society that has stood for hundreds of years. We function well, and these rules have kept us from crumbling and infighting. If we allow one that different to exist, it might break down the world we've worked hard to create."

The king didn't look at Whitney as he spoke easily about ending her life. The same callous disregard for life she saw in Tim's eyes was coming through in their father. Sam must have sensed it, too, as he looked back over to Whitney. She could almost feel his despair. She wasn't about to let him give up.

Without thinking, Whitney pushed herself up, forcing her fin to hold her weight and allow her to stand. It hurt, and felt the pain as a few of her bones cracked, but she wasn't going to just sit in a glass ball waiting to be saved. She was done with that. Grabbing the rim that was barely within reach now, she held on tight as her fin gave out, more bones cracking in the process. She still didn't care. Sam was giving up. She wasn't. She'd fight hard enough for the both of them.

Sam's head snapped to her as soon as the first bone crunched and he didn't hesitate to run over to her when her fingers wrapped around the glass rim of the bowl. He ripped his shirt off in the process and threw it over the glass edge.

Whitney realized her hands were being cut by the glass. Not only did they make it so you had to break your fin to get out, you would cut your hands in half at the top if you did reach it. She hadn't thought of that. The glass looked normal to her, but as blood dripped down the inside of the bowl, she couldn't get out.

Sam's shirt was there as he helped her move her cut hands over. He was standing just a little taller than the bowl, and when she looked down, she saw it was water holding him up, and the water in the bowl had moved to hold her in a seat also. She still needed to learn that ability.

"Neat trick," she said quietly as they stood there face-to-face.

"You need to get back down in that water and let your hands and fin heal," he told her, or rather ordered her.

Whitney grinned. Sam was just so Sam. She was anxious about what was coming, but that didn't seem to matter in that exact moment. She was there with Sam. Everything she had been thinking and worrying about flew out the window. She was getting one last chance with him and was too tongue-tied to say anything. Snapping out of it was hard, but she needed to talk to him.

"I can't let you take all the blame for this. You aren't a bad guy for saving my life. This isn't how it's supposed to end," she complained.

She couldn't help it. Whitney had spent her whole life on the outside of the skinwalker clan, one of them but never fitting in. She never had a boyfriend or fell in love. Never in a million years did she think this going to be her world, but now it was, and she didn't want to let go of it.

Sam genuinely smiled as he finally pried her hands off, and she let go of the glass and put her cut hands into the water she was sitting on. She could feel the cuts heal back together. Normally something like that would awe her, but now it just made her sad. Here she sat, completely okay, and he was going to get punished, and maybe even surrender his life for being a good guy.

He reached for her face and touched it.

"I didn't want you here and part of this world. You see the good in everything. You come from night humans that are raised to protect. That isn't this world. I just want you to be able to go home and live your life. I don't want you caged here." He was back to being sad.

"Do you honestly think I want to go back to a world where you aren't?"

Sam's eyes lit up. Without hesitation, he leaned over the edge of the glass and crushed his lips to Whitney's. He pulled back only a fraction and whispered to her, "Are you sure about that?"

Sure? Absolutely! Sam made her life have purpose again. He brought her back to where she was meant to be. No, she didn't want to be without him.

"If you are sure, then I think I can fix this," he whispered in her ear as he trailed kisses down her neck to hide his words to her.

Her face would have shown surprise if she wasn't turning red from all the stares of the people watching them. Pulling his face back to hers, the make-out session was now a way to get a few last words in.

Whitney leaned forward and ran her healed hands through his hair, making it so that she could lean forward and whisper to him.

"Then how do we get out of here?"

"The answer is in the water," Sam replied, the statement not telling her much. "If you love me, then the water will save us," he whispered back to her.

Whitney pulled back from his kisses and gazed into his eyes. She had no idea what his plan was, and he was obviously not going to elaborate.

"Trust me. I can get us free." He nuzzled into her neck before moving back to her lips for one last kiss.

Whitney melted into his lips. It was perfect to kiss Sam

and always would be. She could feel it in her heart. Sam was her future, and there wouldn't be one without him. She trusted him, even if she would have liked a few more details. It was crazy, as she liked to be the one in control and fighting, but because she didn't know how to play the game she was useless. She was going to push down all instincts to fight and trust him completely. You have to trust in love, her mother had told her as a child, and now she finally understood. She loved and trusted Sam.

"Stay in the water, and we'll be fine," he instructed. "No matter what they do to me or how bad it might look like it feels, don't leave the water."

Whitney knew others could hear him now, so his words were covered in code. She didn't like being told what to do, but she would do what he said now. The look in his eyes told her that he had a plan, and she was ready for anything.

Sam leaned down one last time and kissed her. It wasn't a passion-filled kiss, but one of confidence.

"I love you, Whitney," he declared for her and everyone there watching them.

Whitney gaped in shock. She couldn't say anything back because it had been unexpected, but as he marched away, she felt it in her heart. She was completely in love with him, too, and would tell him as soon as she got the chance, and not in front of hundreds of people hanging on their every word. Power surged through her as she admitted that much to herself and knew that he loved her too.

CHAPTER 11

Sam walked away from Whitney, and it was the hardest thing to do. He had a plan, and he was certain it would work, as long as she actually did what he said and stayed in the water. She had proven time and time again that she didn't like to be ordered around, but he hoped for both their sakes she could set that aside now. His plan would only work if she could listen for a change.

Standing before his father, he bowed his head.

"I believe I was destined to find Whitney and that she belongs with the sirens. I ask that I stand trial by fire to prove that the gods approve of her and wish her to be here. If I survive, I want to have her as my mate, and I'll take full responsibility for her and teach her everything about being a siren," Sam told his father, head still down so he couldn't watch for his reaction.

He wasn't sure how his father would take his declaration, but he needed to make a bold move. While Sam wasn't a believer in the gods that the sirens believed in, the sirens' faith might help them. That was the only way to keep her safe and to keep her out of Tim's hands. If his father deemed it a message from the gods, they would be safe, and Sam wouldn't have to fight for the right to be her mate.

His father pressed his fingers together as he stared at Sam. After what seemed like forever, but was probably just minutes, the king nodded.

"So be it. Trial by fire it is."

Whitney sat in her bowl with the water now clouded a bit from her bloody hands. She was fine, even though she was shocked. He had hoped she wouldn't understand what was going on, but it seemed she understood enough. Trial by fire did seem quite self-explanatory.

Several men moved to the stage and began a fire in the pit off to the side. Sam stood and watched, knowing it was going to be extremely painful, but that didn't matter much. He'd dealt with more pain over his young life than both the men making the fire combined. You didn't get a head guard position without a little pain. *What's a little more?*

Whitney stared at him, and his gaze immediately found hers. The shock on her face was gone, and she was giving him her "what's going on now" face. Sam nodded to her, hoping to reassure her that it would all be fine. That didn't last long as Tim hopped up on the stage and offered to help their father, who was getting down from his chair and handing his shirt to his mother.

Sam didn't look at his mother. Behind her queenly composure, she would be terrified. She had already given him an earful twice since he returned to the island. First, she was upset about the position he was in. She told him several times that she raised him better than making rash choices. Then she was upset that he would keep such a lovely girlfriend from meeting her. She was the only one that knew Sam planned to choose a life alone rather than find a mate, and she didn't blame him. She didn't like any of his choices on the island, either. While she only spoke with Whitney for minutes, Whitney had completely won over his mother.

Sam's father waved him over to the slab of rock that was fitted with metal chains. Sam nodded and sat down where he needed to be. Laying back on the rock wasn't comfortable, but it was going to be fine. He needed to keep repeating that to himself. If his confidence wavered at all, he was sure Whitney would do something reckless.

Tim hovered over him, stepping on his hand as he reached to buckle Sam's right arm. Sam wanted to say something, but knew Tim was doing it on purpose to get a rise out of him. Sam kept his mouth shut and didn't look at him.

"What, no goodbye for your loving older brother?"

It wasn't going to be a good-bye, but he wasn't about to tell Tim that. Tim hovered close, trying to read his face. Sam still didn't look at him; he only gazed at his father as he stood there. The king wasn't a large man. In fact, many of the sirens were larger than him, but what his father had wasn't in physical strength. It was the power of his voice. Sam's mother had told him over and over again that Sam was the son he had always wanted, but Sam doubted that much. He had the same control as his father, but he didn't have the desire to hurt people like him. The king watched as Tim buckled him down, knowing full well that Tim was trying to bruise him up before the test began, and yet he said nothing. That was the king as a father. If it didn't hurt, than it didn't make you stronger. Sam was younger than five when he first found that out and nothing had changed.

As Tim got the last chain hooked up, he knelt down beside Sam.

"Don't worry, little bro. When you're gone, I'll make sure Whitney is well taken care of. She's quite the beauty and has curves in just the right places. Oh and the attitude is perfect. You know I like my girls with a bit of fight in them. She's just what I've been looking for. Thanks so much for taking care of finding me the perfect siren."

Tim grinned, yet Sam still didn't respond. It took a lot of control not to look back or break the chains holding him to hit his brother for even looking at Whitney. Luckily, Sam had self-control in abundance. Sam continued to stare at his father and ignore the words of Tim. He could always hit him later. After only a moment, Tim saw he wasn't getting a rise out of Sam, and he got up and sulked away. Sam didn't dare let out the breath he was holding in case Tim decided to come back and taunt him some more. Whitney was the hardest subject for Sam to keep a clear head about, and now was the time above all others that he needed to keep a clear head.

The king turned to the audience at hand. It seemed like more people trickled in as the fire was being started and word got around the island that Sam chose trial by fire. They were getting past sitting and the new people had to stand at the back. That was a good thing, as the more people saw of it, the more they would accept Whitney with her pink tail.

"We are gathered together here to see what the fates have decided," Sam's father said quietly, and the crowd instantly shut up. "My son, Samuel, has claimed the gods want our siren clan to have a new member— one he was fated to create. He has offered to prove it with trial by fire and I, on behalf of the gods, accept it. Let us test the fates and see if we have a new member or not."

Sam glanced at Whitney one last time. As his eyes were sweeping over the crowd, his father's words finally set in for Tim. Without Sam, Whitney wasn't going to join the siren. Tim seemed upset, and that almost made Sam smile. His eyes finally found Whitney, and his heart was instantly uplifted. She looked scared for him, and he wished he could have told her more. So far she was still in the water, and he hoped she would stay there. Sam nodded to her as she placed a hand on the glass like she was reaching out for him. He opened his hand to her, reaching also and wishing she could be beside him.

One of the men from the fire brought over a pail and handed it to the king. Sam turned back to watch his father. He needed to be sure not to draw attention to Whitney.

"Samuel, transform," his father ordered him. "You are not allowed back in your day human form until I tell you so."

The king didn't need to use any force in his voice even though he did. Sam was willing to play the game and ready. His blue fin appeared beneath the chains, and he waited, watching the man he had grown to hate over the years. It was appropriate that his dad was the one to deal out the punishment.

The king stood above Sam, part man, part siren. The tattoos covering the king's body had been placed identical to his siren form, and almost seemed to be swirling in the light of moon on his skin. Sam's father was more king than father now as he stood above him. He didn't look at what he was doing or if Sam transformed like he ordered. His eyes were locked with Sam. Surprisingly, for once in his life, Sam saw hesitation. Maybe there was more father than king there. Even though Sam had waited his whole life for his father to be a father over being the king, he didn't need a fatherly moment. He needed to save Whitney.

"I'm ready to prove she belongs here. I am ready to prove my act was sanctioned by the gods," Sam added, trying to make sure his father went through with it. The king snapped out of his hesitation and nodded.

Without any more thought, the king dumped the bucket of burning coals on Sam's fin.

Whitney watched as hot coals dropped all over Sam's beautiful blue fin. The iridescent blue scales scalded and immediately flaked off of him. Steam came off the flesh as it burned. She had a feeling that was what was coming, but it was still a shock. A sick charred smell came from where Sam was chained down, almost like the smell of cooked fish that she had once hated the smell of. She was never going to like the smell now. Whitney turned to the queen, hoping his mother would stop it, but the lady was glued to her chair, her face a mask of no concern. Then Whitney felt it. Her tail was beginning to welt up.

'Don't scream or make a sound,' Sam's voice came through her mind.

Whitney's face snapped up from examining her fin to Sam across the stage. He wasn't looking at her; he still had his eyes locked on his father with his mouth clenched shut. She must have imagined him speaking.

Like it had with her hands, the water instantly healed the blisters. But that was short lived. Again they formed with just as much pain as the first time. The cycle repeated.

Whitney looked back at Sam. She was positive she had just heard his voice in her head, and he knew what was going on. Whitney raised a hand to knock on the glass to get his attention.

'Don't draw any attention to you. If I leave this completely unscathed, they will all think it's the work of the gods. We can't let them know we're bonded already,' he clarified.

The blisters healed over and then reformed. They kept the cycle on repeat as Sam laid there on the rock. The only way he wasn't dead now or screaming in agony was that the same healing was happening to him. More than enough scales had flaked off to be burning more than just the outer layers if he hadn't healed.

Then it hit her. He had just told her they were bonded. That was impossible. She never chose to bond to him. That had something to do with blood sharing and loving the other person. She only knew bits from her upbringing, but she was pretty sure that when you bonded to someone, you had to know it was happening. Yet, the blisters appeared and disappeared on her own fin.

'I sensed it days ago, but I didn't know what I was feeling. After talking to my mother a little, I was sure a bond was what I felt,' Sam explained calmly, even though he still had to be feeling excruciating pain from the continuous burning.

Whitney stared at him, not comprehending. First off, he was talking in her head. How was that possible? Night humans could talk to each other silently, but they had to be touching. He was over fifteen feet away from her. Second, all this stuff of bonding was impossible. She had never agreed to bond to anyone. A night human bond was basically like marriage without divorce. She would have definitely remembered saying yes to something like that, or if Sam had mentioned it. She was too young to get married. Bonding was not in her future any time soon. And third, she saw and now felt the burning of the coals on Sam's fin. How the heck was he able to talk calmly to her as the pain raced through them both?

Sam lay on the slab of rock and continued to stare at his father. The cycle continued, blisters, pain, healing, repeat. Whitney felt everything he was feeling, but she had a good sense that his was much more painful as the blisters had to transfer to her and she had to heal them before he would heal. He didn't move a muscle or make a sound. He laid there and took his punishment in front of everyone.

'I'm guessing bonding isn't common for skinwalkers?' Sam asked, sensing her confusion.

'No, the skinwalkers all bond. But I never paid attention to all of that. They bond skinwalker to day human witch,' Whitney explained. Yep, it was just like talking with night humans touching. At least that part she could kind of understand.

'Then why is all this confusing?'

'Because witches are female, and I was a skinwalker. I never expected to find a mate. I only once met a male witch, and he tried to kill me. So, no, I never learned much about bonding because I didn't think I'd have to know anything about bonding to someone.'

There, it was out in the open. He could take that as he wished. She was still left with hundreds of questions.

'Well, you have one now. I hope you aren't disappointed.'

Disappointed? She just got the hottest guy in school as her boyfriend, and now, somehow, he said he was her mate. That wasn't something to be disappointed about. She was just plain old confused by everything, but not disappointed about it.

Whitney felt relief from him, and that made her stare

harder at him. His face was still set in stone, and he was watching his dad as his dad watched him. How could she feel his relief? For that matter, why would he even feel relief?

'I guess I should explain the bond a bit while we sit here and get fried,' Sam joked. Whitney wanted to scold him and would have if it wouldn't bring attention to her. *'To bond, all you need is to exchange blood and love someone. I had fed on you the day I saved your life with my blood. We exchanged blood that day, and within enough time to form a bond. We must have both had feelings for each other since I think the bond formed right away. We just didn't realize that was what we were feeling.'*

'But I didn't even love you then.' That might have been a stretch. She had a crush on him for over a year and loved her swimming lessons alone with him when she could flirt all she wanted, but that wasn't love. That was a crush.

'I don't think you have to know that you love the person for the bond to work. I mean my father forces people to bond if their parents arrange it. They don't exactly love each other, but the bond forms anyway.'

'Yeah, Noah said that, too, but I can't exactly agree with that. The only thing I really knew about bonds was that you had to love the person for it to work. There is no way your father, magical voice or not, could make me love someone.'

'Then Noah did find you? Why aren't you running back home to the skinwalkers right now on the first plane out of Florida?' Now there was anger inside him, too. That was strange to feel, because Whitney didn't feel angry about staying. In fact, she was happy she had stayed.

'Noah did what I told him to do. You can't be mad at him. Now finish explaining the bond before this is all over, and I have to pretend to know what is going on.'

'Fine, but that doesn't let him off the hook. He was supposed to save you.'

Whitney rolled her eyes at him. This all was a bit surreal.

He was being burned by hot coals and having a conversation with her at the same time. And she was rolling her eyes. She just couldn't help it. If she didn't want to hear more of an answer, then she would have added *"fine, Dad"* to the conversation to emphasize her point.

'The bond is mental and physical,' Sam continued his explanation like they were having a nice conversation. *'We share pain and wounds now. That's how I knew this would work. When you cut your hands on the bowl, I felt it, too. If you hadn't healed them as quickly as you did, then I would have been bleeding also, and everyone would have known we're already bonded. This way, they can watch in awe when my father is done and think this is all divine intervention saving me and making you one of us. The sirens believe heavily in their gods and will accept you if they think you were sent by the gods.'*

That was a flawless plan. Again, Whitney had a lot to learn. The mer world was part of the night human world, but there was so much in her upbringing she hadn't learned. It was true she never thought she'd get a mate, so she didn't pay attention to any of that. Now she had one, and she wasn't quite sure what to make of it. He was lucky that she did love him or she would have been protesting.

'And I love you, too,' he said in her mind.

Whitney stared at him. She hadn't sent those thoughts to him.

'Part of being bonded means we share more than just what you send to me.'

Whitney's mouth dropped open. Yes, she really needed to read up more on the whole night human bond thing. Would her mind ever be her own? That wasn't something anyone ever told her about being bonded.

'I'll have my mother teach you how to shield your thoughts, and I promise not to eavesdrop if I can help it.'

'You better,' Whitney threatened him as new welts formed and melted away. A second idea quickly came to her

as she watched them cycle through, appearing and disappearing. If he could read her thoughts, maybe she could read his.

'Don't even try,' he told her. *'It would be a waste of your time since I already shield my thoughts to keep my father out when he questions me.'*

Great. That opened up a whole other problem. She never thought to ask if the siren king could look into the minds of sirens like the alpha of the skinwalkers could. She had grown up connected to the alpha. Would that be the same now?

'I don't think he can connect to you. That's why he suggested killing you. My father is the kind of person that likes complete control. If he can't control you, then you are a problem.'

Sam's words ended abruptly, and Whitney looked up at him from watching the welts on her own fin heal.

The audience stared at Sam as he was tortured by his own father. It seemed to last forever, but it couldn't have been more than ten minutes. When the older man finally thought Sam had enough, he picked up all the burning coals with tongs, one by one. Ordering someone to grab a bucket of ocean water, the king washed away the last of the ash off Sam's fin with salt water that should have stung if the wounds were still there. The blue color sparkled as the moon glinted off Sam's wet tail.

"As you can all see, the gods have found favor in my son and his decision. He has brought us a gift in the form of a new siren."

The king turned knowing eyes to Whitney and nodded his head to her. She was pretty sure he understood what had happened even if he couldn't get into her head. With a flick of his finger, she was pushed right out of the bowl, floating on the water she sat in. She ended up next to Sam, who had already freed himself and was sitting up on the slab. Her pink fin shook at little as she looked his own fin over to make sure there still wasn't a cut on it. She already knew it was better, though she couldn't help but to look. The queen had stood up and brought a sheet to wrap around her, indicating she should change back. Whitney was grateful that at least one person remembered she was completely nude.

The people all stared at Whitney, still showing a bit of hostility and confusion. Sam stood up on his transformed legs and pulled her with him, wrapping his arms around her to keep the sheet tightly concealing her body from everyone as she transformed also.

"As it's my eighteenth birthday today," he told everyone as he looked around. "I am making my choice of a mate. I choose Whitney."

Shock lined the faces all around them except for a few. Behind the normal mask, a small smile slipped at the corners of his mother's mouth. His father also, while keeping a neutral face, seemed to smile with his eyes. There were a few that weren't happy by the news. Tim was in the front row scowling, and a few rows behind him sat Amber wearing the same look of disgust. But Whitney didn't let that bother her. In fact, it was a bit hard to listen to anything as she stood completely naked except for the sheet wrapped around her. One of her worst nightmares growing up had been to arrive to class naked, and now she stood before a whole audience of the clan she just joined wearing almost nothing. Not the best welcoming.

Soon enough the shock wore off the crowd, and the people began to cheer around them. Even though Sam seemed to dislike the island, Whitney could see the people on the island did like him. In fact, they stared a bit with admiration at him, maybe now more than before because he had survived his trial by fire. Some even openly gaped at him like he had been blessed by the gods as his father declared. Sam was correct that they all took it as a sign that she was meant to join them even if he did really just trick them all. Sam took Whitney's hand from beneath the sheet and held her tight in his arms.

"What happens next?" she asked, still not sure of what she had gotten herself into.

Sam nibbled on her ear, obviously not shy of public displays of affection. All the people watched them, and Whitney's face turned a bit red. She had hoped after his announcement they would all leave, but they sat there watching them like they were a great TV show instead.

"We exchange a little blood and pretend to bond, and then we party. All mer love a celebration," he said softly into her ear. "And then we slip away so that I can welcome you to my world without all the distraction, maybe give you a personal tour of the island and show you where we will be living together when we come to visit this place, or we are requested back by my dad."

His voice made her shiver, and that got an even bigger grin from him. Pulling her hand up to his lips, he kissed it. Sam's dark eyes twinkled almost like the stars above them. She didn't need to hear more words to feel the love he had for her. The bond was telling her exactly what he was feeling.

And just like that, her life had changed. What started off as a normal senior year in high school was turning out to be life-changing, and not just because she was going to be eighteen soon and legally an adult. Whitney was once again a night human, and she wasn't sure what was going to come next. They had much left to sort out, but she was going to enjoy doing just that. Moving to Florida turned out not be so bad after all. She had felt alone for so long, but she didn't any more. She had a mate and a very dysfunctional family and clan to belong to now. Life was sure going to stay interesting, but she was more than happy to welcome it. Meeting Sam as a kid was fate, and she was glad she had met him then and now. He was meant to be in her life, and she was meant to be in his. That was the only thing Whitney was certain about now.

5555555555555555555

Sam pulled his lips from her hand and gave her a smile brighter than the full moon in the sky. "Welcome to the mer world, princess."

ACKNOWLEDGEMENTS

To you, the reader. <u>Thank You</u> for taking the time to read this story. If you liked it, please leave a review on your favorite online bookseller (or all of them!) and connect with me social media. The greatest help you can do to keep a writer going is to support them by spreading the word about their books.

Also I would like to thank my editors and cover designers. A good editor is essential to getting the story correct (and in my case- several). Thank you so much, Kathie at Kat's Eye Editing, Melissa at There for You Editing, and Ashton Brammer. They work so hard to get you guys the best book. A thank-you to my *AMAZING* cover artist Jessica for such a pretty cover- doesn't she do great work!! I'm beyond fortunate to have found these wonderful professionals to work with.

I'd also like to thank my hubby – who is the only reason I actually even published. He gives me time when I need it to work on my stories. He encourages me to keep going each and every day on this adventure. And he does all the behind-the-scenes effort to make this work. This would be so much harder without his help. So thank you, B. for pushing me off the deep end (or the cliff as I see it sometimes). And a great big thanks to my little munchkins who keep me going from before the sun comes up 'til long after it sets. Love you AK, KB, and EM.

<u>Thank you so much for taking the time to read my novel!!</u>

ABOUT B. KRISTIN McMICHAEL

Originally from Wisconsin, B. Kristin currently resides in Ohio with her husband, three small children, and three cats. A former cell biologist, she now does the mom thing of chasing kids, baking cookies, and playing outside while writing full time. She is a fan of all YA/NA fantasy and science fiction. Find her at www.bkristinmcmichael.com and Twitter, Facebook, Instagram, and Goodreads under B. Kristin McMichael.

BOOKS BY B KRISTIN MCMICHAEL

- To Stand Beside Her

Chalcedony Chronicles
- Carnelian
- Chrysoprase
- Aventurine
- Chrysocolla

The Night Human World series:

The Blue Eyes Trilogy (series 1)
- The Legend of the Blue Eyes
- Becoming a Legend
- Winning the Legend

The Day Human Trilogy (series 2)
- The Day Human Prince
- The Day Human King
- The Day Human Way

The Skinwalkers Witchling Trilogy (series 3)
- The Witchling's Apprentice
- The Wendigo Witchling
- The Witchling Seer

The Merworld (series 4)
- Water and Blood
- Songs and Fins (coming soon)